MISS DELACOURT HAS HER DAY

Other books by Heidi Ashworth:

Miss Delacourt Speaks Her Mind

MISS DELACOURT HAS HER DAY

•

Heidi Ashworth

AVALON BOOKS
NEW YORK

© 2011 by Heidi Ashworth
All rights reserved.
All the characters in this book are fictitious,
and any resemblance to actual persons,
living or dead, is purely coincidental.
Published by Avalon Books,
an imprint of Thomas Bouregy & Co., Inc.
160 Madison Avenue, New York, NY 10016

Library of Congress Cataloging-in-Publication Data

Ashworth, Heidi.
  Miss Delacourt has her day / Heidi Ashworth.
     p. cm.
  ISBN 978-0-8034-7716-2 (acid-free paper)
  I. Title.
  PS3601.S58M54 2011
  813'.6—dc22
                                            2010031076

PRINTED IN THE UNITED STATES OF AMERICA
ON ACID-FREE PAPER
BY HADDON CRAFTSMEN, BLOOMSBURG, PENNSYLVANIA

Acknowledgments

Many thanks to the talented James Blevins for graciously allowing me to use the lovely poem he penned for his beloved Rebecca. Sir Anthony couldn't have said it better.

Special thanks to Dedee, Jami, Jen, Laura, and Shirley; my supersmart and supportive critique group. Thank you also to my husband and children, who gamely refrained from critiquing the state of our home while this book was being written. Thanks to Becky for being the first to suggest I write a *Miss D* sequel and to Mom for asking me to write another book. I dedicate this to all of you as well as those below who have been kind and generous with my writing. Look for some version of your name in this book: Becky, Bud, Carolyn, Debbie, Dedee, Hillary, James, Jami, Jana, Jen, Karen, Kimberly, Laura, Marilyn, Pam, Pat, Rebecca, Reed, Roxanne, Scott, and Shirley.

Prologue

Sir Anthony Crenshaw was the happiest of men. Less than a week previous he had been assured that the love of his life, the ingenuous Ginny Delacourt, would be forever fastened to his side. Their whirlwind courtship, which began with what was to be a day trip to the country at the behest of his grandmama, turned into a two-week pox quarantine replete with miscommunication, mishap, and mayhem at the country estate of Squire Barrington. Now that he and Ginny were betrothed, their courtship was finally at an end, and, for the first time in his life, his life could begin. He owned that being wed to Ginny promised to be wholly different from the staid and socially sterling existence he had heretofore known, but she would certainly make existing more interesting. In point of fact, he meant to make never being parted from her his life's work.

A trip to London would be necessary to shop for bride clothes and acquire a special license, but the remainder of the short weeks between their betrothal and the wedding would be spent at Dunsmere, his grandmama's country estate, where he and Ginny planned to be joined as man and wife in the rose garden. At this very moment, all that was wanted was for his beloved to enter through the door of the salon, where he waited to take her into dinner, and then to walk among the roses, where they could enjoy another blissful evening out from under Grandmama's sagacious gaze.

Why, then, did he feel such a presentiment of doom when the butler entered and placed a thick letter, the address scratched out in a familiar chicken scrawl, into his outstretched hand? The vellum inside was sure to be replete with more of the same, and since the author rarely had anything to say that promised even a hint of good news, Sir Anthony was tempted to toss the whole of it, unopened, into the fire that burned merrily in the grate. The thought that the composer of this ominous epistle, though in and of himself a harbinger of doom, rarely committed his nay-saying to paper and ink stayed his hand. Reluctantly, he broke the wax indented with the seal of the seventh Duke of Marcross and took in the shockingly brief message.

Tony,
  Reed is dead. Come at once.
                                              Marcross

Reed dead! Sir Anthony thrust the letter with shaking hand into the fire as he should have in the first place. As tragic as it was for his cousin, a man in the prime of life, to have met his end so suddenly, it was tantamount to disaster for Sir Anthony. He would mourn Reed's death, but he would mourn the demise of his own freedom that much more. Just a moment ago he had been himself, Sir Anthony, a man free of any constraint except for that of impending wedded bliss. Now, he walked from the room with feet like lead, as *Crenshaw,* the recalcitrant heir to death, duty, and the Duke of Marcross.

Chapter One

Sir Anthony Crenshaw was once again impatient. He had been cooling his heels in the ghastly Egyptian-inspired antechamber of his uncle's ducal domicile for the better part of an hour. Could it have been little more than a fortnight since he had waited, in like agitation, for his grandmama to grace him with her presence? It seemed as if his entire life had occurred since the momentous day he had been requested to escort one Miss Delacourt on a simple journey. At the same time, it seemed as if only a mere hour had passed—the one shared, stare for stare, with the statue across the way. It had the body of a man with a head of a crocodile, and if he had been caught in its briery maw, his current quandary couldn't feel less thorny.

If only his cousin, Reed, were here! He knew just how to handle his plaguey father. But Reed was dead and no longer able to stand buffer between Anthony's carefree existence and the Duke of Marcross. Indeed, his uncle's imminent death was all that remained between Anthony's freedom and the onerous weight of a dukedom, a role to which Reed had been born and bred. Gad, the gods were cruel! If anyone doubted, they need spend only a moment gazing into the statue's crocodile grin.

"His Grace will see you now."

Startled by the footman's silent entrance, Anthony jerked his head out of his hands. Apparently his hair had been twisted in his fingers, for his scalp now hurt like the devil. No matter; at least his silent communiqué with the golden statue was at an end. It seemed God did grant small favors. Sadly, Anthony was persuaded he was still going to need a large one.

With a growing sense of foreboding, he rose to his feet and followed the footman into the master chamber, where his uncle could be found propped up in a massive bed adorned with red and black satin swags against bedposts fashioned into barley twists and topped with the heads of jackals. Anthony shuddered. The jackal represented the death-god Anubis, a fact that disturbed him never more than at this moment. A man's bed, particularly that of a duke, should be about life and progeny and family, not death! It would never do for Ginny, his betrothed. He dreaded the day they would be expected to sleep in it. Not for the first time, he said a silent prayer that his uncle would make a miraculous recovery. Zeus! He would pray for his uncle's immortality if he thought it even a remote possibility.

The man was indeed sick. Anthony attempted to gauge his uncle's mood based on the expression in his watery eyes but noted only that they had faded into nothingness against the dark circles underneath. Clearly, he was at death's door, and Anthony feared that Ginny's plans for a June wedding were all but in the basket. And so would Anthony's entire day if the irascible duke was in one of his moods.

"Your Grace, I am entirely at your service," Anthony said, hoping he sounded kind rather than exasperated. After all, the man had just lost his son and was, himself, dying.

"Ah! Crenshaw," the duke crowed, "you took your sweet time in getting here!"

Anthony closed his eyes against a particularly insistent wave of annoyance. Time was indeed sweet, and his uncle ate it like candy. Anthony's candy. Yet, it was the "Crenshaw" that nettled him most. It was Reed's title, but Reed's father had dubbed Anthony "Crenshaw" before the dirt had dried on Reed's casket.

Miss Delacourt Has Her Day 5

Opening his eyes, he pasted a smile to his face. "Your Grace, my apologies, but I am here now."

"Well, you ought to be! I waited on you so long, I fell asleep!"

Surely, there was no civil reply to that piece of impertinence. Anthony bit his tongue and waited.

The duke gazed narrowly up at his nephew. "Is that all you've got to say for yourself? Ah! Well, then." He sighed and chewed at his lower lip. "If you had been here in time, you would know that I've just had the doctor in. You might have heard for yourself. I'm dying!"

"My deepest condolences. You have had quite a blow. We have all had."

"Young man, you haven't the slightest idea!" the duke barked. "Losing my only son and heir was punishment enough, but for everything to go to a fop and a fribble such as you . . . Well! I can't think what I have done to deserve such mortification!"

Anthony, who felt sure he could think of any number of sins that would account for his uncle's misery, reached up to adjust his cravat. True, Anthony had heretofore led a somewhat aimless existence, but there was nothing frivolous about paying one's wardrobe the utmost respect.

"Uncle, you have my word, no one is more prostrate with despair over Reed's death than I."

"Is that so? Well, boy, you are about to get your lumps. That girl of yours . . . what is it, Guenevere? Geneva?"

"Ginerva. That is to say, Miss Delacourt."

"Yes, that one!" the duke cried, stabbing a gnarled finger at his nephew. "She won't do!"

Anthony treated his uncle to a frosty glare, one he had never before dared use in his ducal presence. "I don't believe I heard you aright. Miss Delacourt will *do*. Indeed, it is safe to say there is no other who could possibly do as well."

"She is far from duchess material. I'm surprised your grandmother should find her in the least suitable. Now, Reed's widow, Roxanne, there's a woman born and bred to be the wife of a duke!"

"Uncle, you can't mean for me to marry my cousin's widow? Why, I've known Roxanne since she was an infant in swaddling clothes! It would be as if I had married my sister!" Anthony caught a carved Egyptian god staring at him from the corner of his eye and suppressed another shudder. "Besides which, my engagement is a fait accompli." He only hoped Ginny would be more willing to take on the duties of a duchy than he.

"It hasn't been announced. You'll do your duty and do it well. You are a Crenshaw!"

Anthony knew a spark of alarm. "You are serious! But why? Miss Delacourt is perfect for me in every way!" He cast about for some virtue of Ginny's his uncle would deem worthy but came up with virtue only. No doubt her propensity for speaking the truth aloud and her utter lack of regard for the pretentious manners of Society would instantly and totally sink her in his uncle's esteem.

"A penniless, no-name vicar's daughter for the next Duke of Marcross?" his uncle demanded with a swipe at his pointy nose. "I won't allow it!"

Anthony was dumbfounded. He and Ginny had been engaged less than a week when he learned of his cousin's death. In the days since, it had not occurred to Anthony that anyone might find his chosen bride to be one mite less than imminently unexceptionable. A mere baronet at the time of their courtship, he was not obliged to look terribly high for a wife, and in spite of Ginny's connection to his grandmother, his uncle was correct with regard to her lack of standing in Society.

Indeed, if he had not been forced into her company by virtue of a quarantine for the pox in the country home of Squire Barrington, Anthony would doubtless not have given Ginny a second glance. Once he had, however, he was smitten. Now that he had learned to love her, he knew he could never be without her. Staggering to the bedside chair, he fell into it.

"So, you are saying we can't be married?"

"So, you are saying we can't be married?"

"No, Ginny," her Grandaunt Regina, the Dowager Duchess of Marcross, insisted. "You will be married. I will see to that. Only . . . not yet."

Ginny began to pace the confines of her grandaunt's favored room, the study where she had exchanged barbs with Sir Anthony less than three weeks ago. One momentous trip into the country and suddenly they were back at Wembley House to order her wedding gown made up by the best modiste in London. Now this!

"It's Anthony's mother, Lady Crenshaw, isn't it? I am more than perfectly aware she does not like me. Last night after supper she begged me not to give her son's new status as Lord Crenshaw, heir to a duchy, a moment's thought. 'Why,' she said, 'everyone knows that heirs to dukedoms marry nobody vicar's daughters every day of the week!'" Ginny felt hot tears sting her eyes. "She all but said I am not fit for her son, the next Duke of Marcross."

"Do let me handle Deborah," Grandaunt snapped. "She is too much for the likes of you. And sit! Your pacing about has my brain feeling scrambled like two eggs in a pan!"

As it was pointless to cross Grandaunt regardless of one's personal convictions, Ginny obeyed. "It's only that I was hoping to find in her a mother after so long without my own. She makes it more than clear I am not what she wants for her son. Doubtless I am far and wide of the mark of what she desires in a daughter, as well."

"This is not a fate reserved only for connections through marriage, Ginerva. Anthony's dearly departed father was all I could wish in a son, but James, his needle-nosed, hardheaded, black-hearted brother, was born first! And may God rest his soul," Grandaunt muttered, "should he ever have the good sense to die and be done with it."

Ginny tried not to stare at her grandaunt's own needled proboscis, but, alas, it was all she could see. Clearly, apples did not fall far from the tree. Not for the first time, Ginny sighed a prayer of gratitude she had inherited her mother's chestnut curls, large gray-green eyes, and pleasantly snub nose. As ugly thoughts had a way of spilling out via the tongue, she placed hers firmly between her teeth, determined to dwell on how kind Grandaunt Regina had been to her, even if only mostly, since the death of Ginny's sharp-nosed father three years prior.

Grandaunt drew a deep sigh. "It is not Reed's widow, Roxanne, who worries me; it is my son, the duke! Heaven knows he adores Roxanne as his own daughter. Now that Reed is gone and all Roxanne's hopes with him, I fear no one will ever be good enough to be mistress of Haven Hall."

Ginny sprang to her feet. "Grandaunt! Say it is not so! You have said over and over there is nothing with which to be concerned." She resumed her pacing. "That we would be married in the rose garden at Dunsmere come June—that all the preparations, save my gown, were already under way!" Ginny was aware she was beginning to babble, but 'twas better than outright weeping. Grandaunt could not abide weeping, so babble Ginny must. "I am fully aware of Lady Crenshaw's objections, but if you can't handle her, Anthony will!" At least she hoped so. The Anthony of three weeks ago would no doubt bow to his mother's wishes, but the Anthony of today—her Anthony—would never forsake her.

"Ginerva, that is beyond the pale. Of course I can handle Deborah! I wish Anthony's father had never married her, but I have no one but myself to blame for that unfortunate miscalculation," Grandaunt said with a sad little shake of her head. "But that is neither here nor there. She knows better than any-

Miss Delacourt Has Her Day 9

one who butters her bread. She will trouble you no further—you can count on that!"

Turning to the window, Ginny shut out everything but the wished-for sound of Anthony's carriage wheels striking the cobbled street below and thought on Grandaunt Regina's words. Ginny knew Regina Crenshaw, the wife and mother of a duke, to be most formidable, but could she make a woman love her daughter-in-law if she had not the inclination? Somehow Ginny rather doubted even Grandaunt could manage that. Suddenly her stomach clenched, and she turned to the dowager duchess in dismay.

"What did you say?" she demanded, then recovered her manners just in time. "That is, I beg your pardon, Grandaunt, I was not properly attending."

Her grandaunt frowned. "Come away from there. I won't have you seen gazing out the window like some lovelorn maiden. What I said was," she continued, though she did not meet Ginny's eyes, "is that there is one obstacle even I have not the power to overcome."

Ginny felt her mouth go dry. "What? Tell me quickly, I do beg of you!" She must know before she lost her composure. Worse, before she lost her newly found tether on her still-unruly tongue.

"You are young, Ginny. There is no hurry to wed. At least, I trust not. A wedding next spring will do as well as this. In fact, I daresay it will make smooth the path."

Now Grandaunt was the one babbling.

"I do not understand you," Ginny said as calmly as she was able, though her heart pounded in her chest with trepidation. "What are you saying? Why should we wait?"

Grandaunt rustled over to her desk and sat down. Taking her quill from its stand, she bent her head to her work and said, "It is my son, the duke. He does not approve the match. I would make him see how wrong he is, but he never listened to me as a child and, I daresay, never will."

Ginny thought perhaps she had gone blind, so quickly did the tears rush to her eyes at her sense of betrayal. "Grandaunt, not you too?"

Grandaunt slammed down her quill with such force, the parchment skipped and upset the bottle of ink, nearly spilling it all over the large gold-leafed desk. "Of course not! How can you ask? I wish you to marry Anthony as much as do you. More, if it were possible! However, there are the duke's objections to overcome. And even should I accomplish that, he will insist on having his finger in every pie. Better to wait until he is dead."

But what of Lady Crenshaw? Ginny had a sinking feeling that Anthony's mother would be as much an obstacle as his uncle, the duke. As she was a youngish woman who appeared to be in the best of health, there was little hope she would be carried off anytime soon. "Can we not be married secretly? We shall be out in the country. No one need ever know."

"Not in the garden, Ginny!"

"Why not?" she retorted, tears of anger now spilling freely. "I can't see how it is anybody's business but our own!"

"That kind of talk, my girl, will not help your case! The Crenshaws are a religious family. Neither the duke nor Deborah would forgive Anthony for marrying outside of church. His father married in church, his grandfather, his uncle the duke, and even I to his father. First, the banns must be properly read, guests invited, and preparations made for the wedding breakfast afterward. The Crenshaws do nothing by halves, and now that Anthony is to be the next duke, his wedding will be a grand affair—mark my words."

"But, Grandaunt, it is so old-fashioned! Anthony doesn't care for such things. *I* don't care for such things!" Ginny insisted.

"I can see I have sadly neglected portions of your education," Grandaunt said in an ominous tone. "When you marry Anthony, you will become a Crenshaw in word and deed. You will be expected to do things in the manner they always have. It is simply the way it is done. My dear, I am sorry, but this is not a decision that is yours to make."

As Ginny wandered from the room and to her own bedchamber where she might weep in peace, she felt as if all her happiness was slipping between her fingers. For the first time in her life she regretted her upbringing, contented as it was. It was an unworthy thought but no worse than her fervent wish that the duke would find it within himself to die of whatever ailed him. He was said to be on his deathbed, but so was Henry the Eighth before he married wife number five. *And* six. Even if the duke surprised them all and was carried off quickly and with uncharacteristic good grace, there were still Lady Crenshaw's objections to overcome. Ginny knew Anthony's mother to be an impediment to her happiness even if Grandaunt did not.

Unless Ginny could prove that she would make a splendid duchess, all was lost.

Chapter Two

Anthony stared into the eyes of one of the appalling wooden jackals that leered over his uncle's hoary head and contemplated what should be done about the duke's aversion to his chosen bride. He could hardly credit that this was happening, not to the flawlessly correct Sir Anthony. Surely it was far from flawlessly correct to contemplate, however briefly, doing away with the patriarch of one's own family. Why, he hardly recognized himself, and all for a slip of a girl with whom he was barely acquainted three weeks ago. A girl who had thought him a bigot, a bore, and a beast. A girl who had turned him so upside down, he nearly didn't recognize his own life. A girl he couldn't live without, not for a year, not for a week, not even for one more day! He would go this very minute to the office of the Archbishop of Canterbury and obtain a special license. With luck, they could be wed tomorrow.

"Crenshaw!"

Anthony leaped to his feet. "Not now, Your Grace. I must go."

A sinister rasping sound came from the eerie bed. It was more than a few moments before Anthony realized it was his uncle's laughter.

"I can see I have landed you a facer, my boy! So, let us cry pax. Put off announcing your betrothal until the end of mourning for my son. In fact, tell no one. If your Miss Delacourt waits for you and you still wish to marry her after I am dead, I will be powerless to stop you."

Anthony did not want to wait. He did not want to mourn. He did not want to be a duke. He wanted to marry Ginny and take her off on a grand tour of Europe. He wanted to show her Romeo and Juliet's Venice, Caesar's Rome, and Hamlet's Denmark. Most of all, he wanted to give Ginny her wedding in the garden at Dunsmere in June when all the roses were in full bloom. Anything could happen between now and next summer. He had almost lost Ginny in the space of a fortnight, and that was when he was a mere baronet. Young, unmarried, and, dare he add, exquisitely dressed dukes hardly littered the ground, even in London. He shuddered to think of the force of nature unleashed against him by the matchmaking mamas of the world if he failed to marry Ginny forthwith.

"Your Grace, I hope you never doubt my deep respect for yourself and for my dear departed cousin. However, I find I cannot oblige you in this."

"Come, come! If the chit truly loves you, she won't mind. Needless to say, she has much to do in preparing her trousseau. No doubt she is plying her needle even now. The daughters of vicars are required to be good with a needle, are they not?" the duke said with a cackle.

No matter how determined Anthony's attempt, a picture of Ginny sitting meekly by the fire, her flashing needle leaving perfectly neat stitches in its wake while she listened to her father rehearse his latest sermon could not, would not, come to mind. "I really couldn't say," Anthony ground out. "Miss Delacourt is not your ordinary, everyday daughter of a vicar. Blast it all, Uncle!" he said, nearly gripping his already much abused hair. "You know this is neither here nor there. Miss Delacourt is perfectly unexceptionable. Why, her lineage is as proud as my own!"

"Ah! Tut-tut, boy, your lines are noble on both sides, while your vicar's daughter has only m'mother's less than sterling ancestry on which to hang her hat. Perhaps you did not know; her grandaunt—*your* grandmother—is descended from a long line of street vendors from Swansea!"

Anthony gazed down at his uncle with revulsion. "Whether she was descended from cits or not, my grandmother is a true lady. My affianced bride is under her care, under her roof, and under her tutelage. If that is not enough for you, I wouldn't deign to know what is." Turning on his heel, he strode toward the door.

"Wait!"

Anthony stopped dead in his tracks and turned halfway about. His uncle was a duke, after all. "Your Grace?" he asked, relieved he still remembered how to hide his ire.

"I hadn't realized you were possessed of so much spirit," the duke mused aloud. "You have changed."

Anthony turned to face his uncle, gave him his most disarming smile, and said, "In that, Your Grace, you are most correct." Then he turned and quit the room, slamming the door behind him. He moved as quickly as possible through the hall and down the stairs in order to avoid everyone from his cousin's widow down through his uncle's butler, the upstairs maid, the matched pair of footmen, and on through to the boot boy, most of whom knew him from boyhood, when Crenshaw House on Hanover Square in London had been his favorite haunt. The servants had known him first as Tony, then Anthony, then Sir Anthony, and now the blasted Crenshaw. However, all he wanted at the moment was to be called "my love" and to be with his.

He was relieved when he encountered no one but the butler and that all he handed Anthony with his hat and gloves was a simple "M'lord." He was safely out the door and down the front stair with his foot upon the carriage step when he heard it.

"Tony!"

That voice. How did it have the power to slide into his heart like a shaft of ice after all this time? Slowly he turned, the

Miss Delacourt Has Her Day 15

space between his shoulder blades itching as if he were expecting a bullet in his back at any moment, until, finally, there she was. Rebecca.

She was poised on the step of her own conveyance for all who passed to better appreciate the way the black-trimmed chocolate brown of her travel ensemble played up the copper of her sparkling eyes. Her extremely long honey-blond hair was done up in thick coils pinned under a jaunty little hat. He felt quite sure she had never looked lovelier.

"It *is* you!" she cried loudly enough for the neighbors safe in their homes to hear. In fact, he thought he saw the curtains in more than one window in the house across the square twitch. Funny, it was here at Crenshaw House that he had last laid eyes on her. On these very same steps. Long ago, that night when he had nearly given her a ring.

"Uh, yes, I live here. That is, I, er, live *here*. In London."

She sprang from her perch and with nimble steps was at his side in a trice. "Yes, of course, but I heard you were getting married next month in some backwater town. How delightful to see I was wrong!"

"No! That is, not wrong; I *am* getting married. In fact, we are in town to choose bride clothes."

She smiled at him coyly, no doubt measuring her words lest they escape her highly rouged lips minus the desired effect. Rebecca, the woman with whom he once fancied himself in love, wielded the most innocuous words with such extraordinary results, one often blinked up from the ground, wondering what hit him.

"How charitable you are!" she said with an arch of one fine, dark eyebrow. "Why, I am certain it was my darling father who paid a small fortune for my bride clothes when I married the earl."

The earl, Anthony recalled, was the rich and ancient nobleman Rebecca had become engaged to the very morning after giving Anthony permission to pay his addresses to her. If anyone had sold herself for a parcel of bride clothes, it was Rebecca. The woman was outside of enough! Did she think him still the callow youth who couldn't see past her beauty to her stony heart?

Choosing his words carefully—he did not wish to hide his reproach, nor did he relish a shouting match in the middle of Hanover Square—he said, "Miss Delacourt, my affianced bride, is under the protection of her aunt. It is she who will foot the bill for the clothing, not I. Had I done, it would raise more than a few eyebrows. I am sure you did not mean to imply anything untoward. In fact, I rather think you have run right past implications into outright accusation, but it will never wash. Miss Delacourt is well known in London for her rectitude." Never mind that it was for her self-righteous prudery that Ginny was known; she was *his* prude, and he loved her for it. "Meanwhile, I have rooms of my own I will be inhabiting, while Miss Delacourt stays with her grandaunt."

He turned to leave Rebecca standing in the street, then thought better of it. "Oh, did I forget to mention? Miss Delacourt's grandaunt is better known to you as the Dowager Duchess of Marcross. However, *I* call her Grandmama."

Rebecca—or Lady Derby, as she was styled since her marriage to her well-heeled earl—paled just a little under the faux red of her cheeks, while her eyes narrowed into slits the color of dirty pennies. "How convenient. No doubt Miss Delacourt's provincial friends are wishful of an aunt such as she, one who just happens to be possessed of a grandson with claims to a duchy." She smiled the way she did when she wanted you to believe all was forgiven when she had in fact just begun to condemn. "How clever you are! La! If I had a stain on my gown—a muslin gown, to be sure—a grandmother like yours would be the first person I would think of as having the means to wash it clean!"

Anthony was suddenly filled with the longing to slap a woman, a feeling he had never known before meeting one

Miss Delacourt Has Her Day 17

Lucinda Barrington, a foolish child who had cornered him into a false engagement shortly before he became engaged to Ginny. For a moment he considered doing just as he pleased, but knew that Ginny, in spite of her tendency to become a bit brutal when in a snit, would not approve.

"Ah! I will be sure to tell Grandmama how low your opinion of her has sunk, Lady Derby. She will no doubt find it as amusing as I." Without a backward glance, he swung himself up into his carriage, where his desires vacillated between indulging in a bout of laughter or taking potshots at the buttons in the upholstery with the gun he kept secreted in the carriage.

After being held up by highwaymen on the road a few weeks back, he felt one could never be too careful, especially since he now had Ginny's safety to consider. On the other hand, being possessed of a loaded firearm could prove less than prudent. He was so weary of hearing how Ginny was not good enough for Lord Crenshaw, heir to a title and all of his uncle's vast holdings, that he would happily put a bullet into the next person to disapprove.

He considered turning around and heading straight for Doctor's Commons, the offices of the Archbishop of Canterbury, to acquire a special license to wed immediately but thought better of it. First, he should confer with Grandmama. If anyone knew how to handle this uproar, it was she. Besides which, she already had the wedding preparations well in hand. She had arranged for the banns to be read, both in his parish as well as Ginny's, starting this Sunday. The *modiste* was due at Wembley House to fit Ginny for her wedding gown this very afternoon. Indeed, he would not be surprised to learn that Grandmama had bullied seeds to spring into flowers in the gardens at Dunsmere just in time for the great day.

Of course, if anyone could shed some light on Rebecca's sudden appearance in town, it would be Grandmama. He had thought the shameless Lady Derby to be safely crowing over the provincial misses in her own backwater estate—but wait.

Wasn't it Lord Derby who'd stuck his spoon into the wall this time last year? He groaned. The woman was a widow, and she was now on the hunt for a new husband. After a day such as today, that was all that was needed! No doubt his mother had much to do with Rebecca's landing on the doorstep of Crenshaw House a month before her son's wedding to another woman. His mother would have much to answer for, not the least of which were her unkind words to Ginny the night previous.

Matters were beginning to take an ugly turn. The only possible hope of applying salve to his wounds was time spent with his beloved. With a savage lash of his whip, Anthony was on his way.

The moment the bell rang at Wembley House, Ginny ran down the stairs to the entry hall. Her ladylike attire, a faded-rose sprigged muslin with perfectly matched sash and shoes, was at odds with her desire to spring to the door and open it herself. It took all her forbearance to remain standing by the stair while Garner, the butler, made his sedate way from the pantry where he had been polishing the silver plate. She could not wait one second longer than needful to hear from her sweetheart's own lips that all would be well.

Oh, bother, why must Garner move so slowly? With a sigh, she pressed her lips together. A future duchess did not harry her servants. Or did she? Ginny wasn't sure but was persuaded Grandaunt would read her a lecture on her conduct, regardless.

Finally, the door was open, but Anthony, with his strong, sure stride, did not immediately enter. From her place by the stair, she could just make out the edge of his blue superfine coat, buff pantaloons, and, upon the removal of his high-crowned hat, the sheen of golden hair.

As Anthony was dark of hair, she banished Grandaunt's imagined admonitions to the back of her mind and hastened to the door, where stood Lord Avery and, beside him, his new bride, Lucinda.

"Why, Lord Avery. Lady Avery. Please do come in. What a surprise." Surprise, indeed. They were the last two she expected to see. Not only were they not particular friends of hers despite the time they'd spent together enduring a pox quarantine earlier that month, they were meant to be off on a wedding journey. "I had thought you safely in Brussels by now."

"Brussels!" Lord Avery snorted, handing his hat and gloves to the butler. "It would seem Boney and I had the very same idea!"

"Yes, isn't it marvelous?" Lucinda cried in typical Lucinda fashion. "Napoleon and my darling Eustace are both military geniuses!"

"Oh," Ginny said, faintly. It was most difficult to picture Lord Avery—chin-wobbler, wallower, and weeper extraordinaire—in the same room as Napoleon, let alone the same career. "I hadn't heard he had made it as far as that."

"Well," Lord Avery said with a wink, "he's not quite there yet. In fact, everyone who is anyone has gathered in wait at the Belgium border."

Ginny could never hope to understand Society's fascination with battle. The idea of sitting in a carriage eating luncheon out of a basket while soldiers fought for their lives a few yards away made her flesh crawl. However, she could see that it suited the drama-hungry Lucinda right down to her toes.

"So, why is it you are not there, then?" Ginny asked as she led them upstairs to the gold and green drawing room. "I should think you would love it above all things." And far better for her if these two were indeed in Brussels and not invading the only hour of quiet she and Anthony would have together for several days. She sighed while Lucinda seated herself on the green shadow-striped sofa as if settling in for a long cose.

"Yes, of course, you know me so well, Ginny! Might I still

call you Ginny?" she asked with a brutal batting of her lashes that threatened to dislodge them from their moorings.

Ginny wasn't sure how to respond. In a society wherein a wife rarely referred to her own husband by his given name in public, Ginny wasn't sure what to say. She so much wanted to be unexceptionable in every way; yet it seemed too staid to insist that Lucinda call her Miss Delacourt after all they had been through in the past fortnight: highwaymen, a pox quarantine, romantic entanglements, and a broken engagement or two.

Taking a deep breath and hoping Grandaunt was not standing in her adjacent study with an ear pressed to the wall, she said, "Yes, naturally, you may call me Ginny, as ever."

"And you may call me Lady Avery! Or just my lady, because we are the best of friends, are we not?"

Ginny felt sure Lucinda was incorrect on two counts; close friends called each other by first names if so desired, yet she and Lucinda could hardly be referred to as such. Under the circumstances, the title of Lady Avery was most appropriate. As startled as Ginny was by Lucinda's lofty double standard, she owned it was so like her, she nearly laughed aloud.

"Very well, Lady Avery. Pray, do tell why you have cut short your wedding journey and returned to London."

"Oh, do let *me* say, my darling!" Lord Avery queried with a glance at his wife. His joy soon turned to concern when he took in her suddenly frail appearance. "My darling! Are you about to faint?"

"Yes, Eustace! Can't you see how I am sinking to the floor even as we speak?" Lucinda demanded in a voice far stronger than possible in one so seemingly incapacitated. Fascinated, Ginny wondered what her role in Lucinda's little drama ought to be. She decided to stay put, a decision that afforded her an excellent view of Lucinda's slow and surely feigned descent to the floor while Lord Avery hastened to place a cushion in every spot he reckoned her head might possibly land.

Sadly, he miscalculated, and there was a loud *clunk* as her head slipped between two cushions and bounced off the hardwood floor.

Lucinda's eyes popped open. "Might you not have caught me this time?" she snapped.

Lord Avery hastened to his wife's side and helped her to her feet. "Yes, of course, my darling. It's only that my back is still in agony from the last few times I have done so."

Considering Lucinda's tiny frame, Ginny could only assume the fainting and catching had been going on fairly constantly ever since their elopement four days prior. Poor Lord Avery! He most likely hadn't had any idea what he was getting along with that fatuous smile and generous dowry.

Lucinda fluttered to her seat while Lord Avery reclaimed the cushions from the floor and propped them all around her head in a vain attempt to hold her aloft should she faint yet again.

"That's quite enough, my love," Lucinda said, rapping him soundly on the arm with her fan. "You see, dearest Ginny," she said in a deep, grave voice, "I am in a delicate condition."

Delicate, indeed! Ginny felt no doubt that Lucinda had a delicate figure, delicate features, and, far too often, a delicate understanding of reality; however, four days was not enough for even the most astute woman to ascertain whether or not her family was growing. Yet there sat Lord Avery, smiling like a cat in the cream pot.

"My lady, pardon me for being so bold, but are you sure?"

"Oh, yes! I have never been so happy in all my life!" Lucinda cried, clearly restored to her natural self. "But that's not what we came here to tell you." She looked to her husband and raised an arched eyebrow.

"Miss Delacourt," Lord Avery intoned, "I am afraid we have some very bad news."

Fear clutched Ginny's heart. "Is that why he is late? Anthony, that is. He was meant to be here by now." Suddenly she had visions of a carriage accident, a slip in the mud, a latent illness that had carried him off in death. "He isn't hurt, is he?"

"No, silly, nothing like that!" Lucinda admonished. "I'm afraid it is far worse. Lady Derby is in town."

Ginny blinked. "I'm afraid I don't perfectly understand. Who is Lady Derby?"

"She is a very rich countess," Lord Avery said. "Much like my lovely wife, only she is a widow, just out of full mourning."

"Oh, and, Ginny, she *is* rich! And young as well as beautiful! Only, you already knew that part, because Eustace said she is much like me!"

Ginny took a deep breath, but it didn't make anything clear. "I haven't the slightest idea what she has to do with me, Lucinda—ah, Lady Avery. You will just have to come straight out and tell me."

"Let me tell her, my darling," Lord Avery insisted. "This matter requires a bit of finesse."

"Eustace, of course!" Lucinda agreed. "You tell her all about the finesse, and I will tell her the part about Anthony's being in love with her. Only, I suppose now we should call him Lord Crenshaw, even though it seems awfully poky after having been engaged to him, even though the whole thing was a sham. Pretending is such great fun!" She turned to Ginny and asked, "Don't you think so?"

Ginny had no reply. She was no longer attending to Lucinda, for there in the doorway, his face as white as his cravat, stood Anthony.

Chapter Three

Anthony had never been so happy to arrive at Wembley House, in spite of its being the scene of many an unpleasant lecture from his grandmama. He had never been so eager to see Ginny, to talk with her and share his hopes and dreams for their future. He had never been so full of dread when he opened the door to the drawing room and heard that goose, Lucinda, tell Ginny about his long-distant past.

One look at Ginny's face, pale in the afternoon light, told him everything he needed to know. He strode to her side and took her cold hand in his.

"Ginny, please do not assume!"

She opened her mouth to say something but snapped it shut again when Lucinda jumped up from the sofa and ran to his side.

"Look, Eustace! It is Sir Anthony!"

"Yes, my flower, I see him," Lord Avery soothed.

"Why, we were just discussing you!"

"So I heard, Lucinda," Anthony said coldly.

"La, sir, but you are to call me Lady Avery now. Or, my lady. That would do, as well."

"I am quite aware of your change in status and title, Lady Avery," he said. In point of fact, he was more than well enough aware of everyone's change in status—Lucinda's, his, Lady Derby's—and he was sick unto death of it. Drawing

Ginny to her feet, he said, "Come sit with me on the sofa, my dear, and I will tell you what has happened."

"Oh, famous!" Lucinda said, clapping her hands. "I wish to hear all about it!"

"Not you, Lucinda," Anthony insisted.

"Well! I never!" Lucinda cried and flounced across the room. It was, unfortunately, the side of the room opposite the door, and Anthony was having none of it.

"Ginny, wait right here until I can get rid of that peagoose."

"Peagoose?" Lord Avery shouted. "That is my lady wife you are insulting. I will have you know she is in a delicate condition and is not up to your brand of spitefulness."

"Delicate condition?" *So soon?* He turned to look a question at Ginny, but her eyes were too full of her own lack of answers to address his. Besides, Lucinda had just fainted into a puddle at his feet.

"Oh, my poor darling!" Lord Avery cried, kneeling to crouch at her side. "You, Crenshaw, are a beast! I should call you out for this!"

"You, Avery, are a nincompoop, and I should have put a bullet into you when I had the chance last week!"

Lord Avery's mouth opened and shut like that of a fish gasping its last gasp, and his chin began to wobble.

"Oh, no, you don't!" Anthony commanded. If he never again saw a grown man cry, it would be too soon. "As for you, Lady Avery," he said, addressing the prone figure at his feet, "do you have an inkling what it means to be in a 'delicate condition'?"

Indignant, Lucinda propped herself up on her elbows. "Of course I do, silly! It's what all the new brides say. First they say they are in a delicate condition, and then they say they have never been happier. Not many of them faint, but I decided I would be the fainting kind long before my come-out. Only I didn't have a come-out because I got the pox and—"

"Enough!" Anthony roared, grasping her by the elbow and jerking her to her feet. "Avery, your wife is not increasing!

Miss Delacourt Has Her Day

Rather, she could be, but it is too soon to know, and somehow I rather doubt the two of you have enough wits between you to start so much as a fire."

"How dare you!" Lucinda cried. "I *do* know how to make a fire. I have watched the chambermaids do it any number of times. And as for that other horrendous accusation, I don't believe I have ever been so insulted in my life!"

"My apologies, Lady Avery. I didn't mean to imply that I believe you to be a liar." What he thought of her was far worse and not the least polite to say aloud.

"Liar? Who is calling whom a liar? You, sir, called me fat and old!"

Anthony was completely nonplussed. Had everyone gone mad? If he lived to see such a benighted day ever again, he would poke out his eyes. "Uh, I, that is . . ."

"Lord Crenshaw does not think you are fat, Lucinda," Ginny said, rising gracefully to her feet. "He was merely pointing out that the meaning of the words 'delicate condition' imply you are increasing."

"But, Ginny," Lucinda pouted, "only the old, fat girls are *enceinte*. Surely you have noticed."

"Yes, dear," she said, taking Lucinda firmly by the shoulders and leading her toward the door. "But you are both young and beautiful. Therefore, you cannot be enceinte. Lord Crenshaw knows this as well as I. Is that not so, my lord?"

"Yes! Yes, that's it exactly!" Bless Ginny's heart for getting him so quickly over a patch of very rough ground.

"Now, Lord Crenshaw and I have a few matters to discuss, but thank you very much for your visit," Ginny continued. "It was so lovely to see you both."

Avery, his face restored to its normal shade of cream, took Ginny's hand and gave it a squeeze. "Thank *you*, Miss Delacourt! Perhaps Lucinda and I shall attempt a trip to the Continent, after all!"

"How marvelous! Please do write and let me know how you

get along. The footman will see you out." And without further ado, the peagoose and the hen were out the door.

Anthony collapsed onto the sofa and sighed in relief. "I thought they would never leave!"

"No matter," Ginny said with an airy wave of her hand. "I daresay when I am a duchess, I shall be obliged to entertain any number of lords and ladies."

"True, I suppose you shall, but I was persuaded you cared little about such things."

"But of course I care! It is the duty of a duchess to ensure social success for the sake of her husband, the duke. There is no point in my waiting until I have a title to be proper and correct," Ginny said with an overbright smile.

Anthony felt a spark of dismay. "Ginny, what has Grandmama been saying to you?"

"Nothing! That is to say, she has been tutoring me on my duties as your future wife, and I am very grateful." She returned to the sofa and sat down, forcing Anthony to rise to his feet. He would have momentarily claimed the place by her side he longed for, but she had displayed her skirts so generously, there was but an inch or two left upon the sofa on which to spread his trousers. It was an affectation he had seen employed by Lucinda a hundred times, which was a hundred times too many. Frowning, he remained standing and forced himself to attend to what his beloved was saying.

"As I do not wish to assume anything, perhaps it is best you tell me about Lady Derby," Ginny said, mild as butter.

No censure, no accusation, no objects being hurled at his head . . . Anthony felt as if the floor were shifting beneath his feet. The woman before him seemed an utter stranger. Surely her head had not been turned by the prospect of becoming a duchess?

"Miss Delacourt," he said, longing to call her Ginny but unsure what game she was playing, "it has never been my purpose to keep anything from you." He paused to gauge her reaction to his words, but her face maintained its former appearance of sweet complacency. "Ah, that is to say, if I had thought it of any import, I would have informed you of my past romantic entanglements." Oh, Lord, that hadn't come out right. Surely now she would give him a piece of her mind. And he would be glad of it!

"La, sir, that is all in the past! You were recently betrothed to Lady Avery, but I am not the least troubled by that fact."

"Ginny, it is hardly the same thing! You know my brief attachment to Lucinda was not known to anyone but those of us in the house, and a total sham, to boot." He turned away from her, afraid to see her reaction or, worse, a lack of it, in her face. "It was not so with Rebecca, er, Lady Derby, and if you think others will let the subject die, you are sadly mistaken."

Now he had gone and done it. In his mind's eye, he saw Ginny's adorable face crumple, her eyes shining with unshed tears. He spun about to capture this evidence of her affection—why, it had been eons since they had spoken of love, perhaps as long ago as yesterday!—only to come face-to-face with Grandmama.

"Anthony! Pray tell, what you are doing here?"

He was taken aback. "I believe I was expected, as I have been every afternoon since our return to London." An ugly thought occurred to him. "You haven't had a letter from my uncle, the duke, have you?" He didn't know how one could possibly have arrived before him, but bad news had a way of traveling quickly. Avery and Lucinda were evidence of that.

"Why? Was there something you wished to confess before I have the whole from my son, the duke?" the dowager duchess asked, murder in her eyes.

Anthony resisted the urge to steal a glance at Ginny's face. He knew she would see the act as doubt, and he would rather take a bullet, even one from that fop Avery, than have her see him waver.

"Confess? Why, Grandmama, you imply I have done something unwarranted. I would, however, be remiss if I neglected to inform you of my uncle's opposition to my upcoming nuptials." There, it was out, and he was glad of it. "If you must know, I believe he cherishes a hope I will marry my cousin's widow. Wouldn't that be a provident solution?" he said with as much nonchalance as he could muster. Surely they would see all what was ludicrous in *that* statement!

Surprisingly, they did not. Grandmama's face went deathly white, and the tears he had hoped for from Ginny moments before started in earnest.

His first emotion was one of intense relief. Finally, a sign that she cared! As he hastened to Ginny's side, he wondered if his selfish reaction meant he was some kind of cad. Taking her into his arms, he let her sob, at great length and with startling thoroughness, into the expensive cloth of his favorite Weston coat as penance for his callousness.

"My poor darling," he murmured into her ear. "I hadn't meant to be so blunt. That is, I did mean to say exactly what was on my mind, but I wasn't wishful to make you so desperately unhappy." Surely a tear or two would have been more than enough proof of her love for him, but there was no sign that the deluge would come to a stop. What now? He waggled his eyebrows at Grandmama over the top of Ginny's head.

Grandmama was not so circumspect. She threw her hands into the air and cried, "Would that I knew! Ginny was her usual intrepid self earlier today over luncheon."

"It's only that I wish to be the best duchess I can be," Ginny divulged between sobs.

"Not that again!" Anthony wanted to give her a good shake but fished in his pocket for a handkerchief instead. "Grandmama, what have you said to her?"

"I? What have *I* said to her?" she gasped. "You are the one who reintroduced that nasty bit of news about your uncle. I daresay the talk about Lady Derby was none too pleasing either."

"I am referring to this newfound passion to be a duchess," Anthony demanded, happy to turn attention away from the two most unsettling conversations of his day thus far. This was quickly becoming the third. "She hasn't been herself since I arrived." The way her fingers crept up into the curls at the nape of his neck was also new, but he thought it best not to draw attention to that bit of impertinence. Grandmama might put a stop to it, and he found he rather liked it. Very much, in fact.

"Yes, well, no doubt we can lay the blame for that in your mother's dish, as usual. Deborah makes it more than clear she doesn't have confidence in Ginerva. Not all young ladies are cut out to be a proper duchess, if you must know, Anthony."

"Since when does Ginny have a care for what anyone thinks of her?" Anthony demanded over the sound of renewed sobbing, but he was not to get an answer, for just then there was a rap on the door, and a Madame Badeau was announced.

"Ah, at last!" the dowager duchess sputtered. "You are late!"

"As you say, Your Grace," Madame Badeau said with a shrug of her shoulders. "*Spécialement* if by late you mean early and *attendu* outside this door *pour toujours.*"

Finally, someone who was a match for Grandmama, not to mention a splendid diversion for Ginny. Anthony felt something akin to glee. How he wished he might tarry and see how events unfolded, but it would not do to remain in the room while his beloved was fitted for her wedding gown.

"I will leave you ladies to your work, then." Gently, he drew Ginny from his shoulder and put a finger under her chin to lift her gaze to his. "Come, come, Miss Delacourt, will you not at least smile for me?" She did not reply, and in the end he was forced to make do with regarding her delightfully upturned nose while discreetly whisking away the teardrop that had made its way halfway down her chin; whereupon there was nothing left to do but depart.

Once the door had shut behind Sir Anthony, Ginny almost

fell into another bout of weeping. They all were against her: Anthony's mother despised her; his uncle, the duke, wished Anthony to marry his cousin's widow; and Anthony's rich, beautiful, and eminently available first love had reappeared upon the scene. Nevertheless, she held her tears at bay; a duchess did not whimper like a schoolgirl. At least Grandaunt never did, and she was the most regal duchess Ginny knew. In point of fact, Grandaunt was the *only* duchess she knew.

As Ginny endured being stabbed with the dressmaker's pins and forced to stand agonizingly still for lengthy periods of time, she played through her mind every encounter she had had with lords and ladies, the very ones she had so recently disdained for their airs and graces. Now she fairly envied them their ability to take everything in stride (at least in public—perhaps they were as full of colic when in private, as was Grandaunt Regina) and smile demurely in the midst of every storm. Ginny sensed this was a skill she would need in future. Perhaps sooner. Drawing a breath, one that didn't disturb the multitude of pins speared through the dozens of pleats in the bodice of her mocked-up gown, she asked, "Grandaunt, who exactly is Lady Derby?"

"She is the widow of one Lord Derby, Earl of Derby. Why do you ask?" Grandaunt asked in a light, bantering tone that fooled no one, Ginny least of all.

"Her name is Rebecca, is it not?"

"And what if it is?" her grandaunt puffed as she went around pulling out imaginary imperfections in the hem of Madame Badeau's most recent work.

"It's nothing really, only that Lord Crenshaw mentioned her. I think it best if I stay abreast of who is who in London this season."

Grandaunt Regina straightened and treated Ginny to a piercing glare. "Ginerva Delacourt! Since when is my grandson 'Lord Crenshaw' to you? And why this sudden interest in titles and who is who? We have a copy of *Burke's Peerage* for that!" Her eyes narrowed, and she pursed her lips. "What has gotten into you?" she mused aloud, more as if she were addressing the question to herself than to Ginny.

"Why, Grandaunt, haven't you been pleading with me to learn the ways of Society? Now that I am ready to do so, you do not like it. I do believe you are getting forgetful," she said in a teasing manner she hoped would sweeten her words a little. Heaven forfend she tell the truth and admit she was petrified that Anthony might cry off and marry his cousin's widow or, worse, Lady Derby, if she did not win his uncle's approval.

True, a gentleman, unless roped into it by the likes of the former Miss Barrington, did not cry off from an engagement, and Anthony was nothing if not a gentleman. However, there would be few to demur should he choose a more suitable lady over an insignificant vicar's daughter. Did the upper crust of society not refer to a short-lived scandal as a seven-days' wonder? If Anthony cried off, it would be but a seven-*hours'* wonder, she had no doubt.

"Oh, Grandaunt," she cried, "what am I to do?"

"Madame Badeau, please leave us," Grandaunt ordered.

"But, Your Grace, *la jeune femme* is full of pins, *encore!*"

"I am well aware of this," the dowager duchess hissed through her teeth. "Retire to the kitchen, and bespeak yourself a cup of tea. You may return when you have drunk it."

"Humph!" was all Madame Badeau had time to say before she was hastened out the door.

Madame Badeau had spoken the truth with regard to the pins holding Ginny's garments together, and Ginny remained still, as any sudden move could bring sharp disaster to her sensitive skin. Nevertheless, she jerked in surprise when her grandaunt returned to her side and tenderly placed a hand on Ginny's cheek.

"Heaven knows it took long enough, but I love you just the way you are, Ginerva Delacourt. And, more to the point, so does *he*."

Tears sprang to Ginny's eyes. "Thank you, Grandaunt, but we both know it is not enough."

Chapter Four

Madame Badeau had been long departed and Ginny was dressing for the evening's engagements—a soiree and two routs—when there came a rap at the door.

"Nan, do please see to that," Ginny asked the young girl who had been securing Ginny's curls so that they bounced around her head à la Caro Lamb.

Nan spat out a mouthful of pins into her hand and ran to the door. Ginny sighed and repressed a desire to scold the girl, who was not a servant at all and truly couldn't be expected to have refined manners. She had come to live with Ginny and her father many years ago and would have had no place to go if Ginny hadn't brought her along to Grandaunt's as her "lady-in-waiting" upon her father's death little more than three years ago.

In the past, Ginny wouldn't have cared two pins about Nan's manners nor her skills as an abigail, but she found that her need to be unexceptionable in every way in the eyes of her future mama-in-law was making her highly critical. However, when Nan placed a piece of thick, folded paper into her hands, she forgot about everything but what it might contain.

With trembling fingers, Ginny slid her finger beneath the heavy wax seal imprinted with an ornate letter *C* and opened the creamy parchment folds to reveal a pair of verses. Her heart skipped a beat; the works of Shakespeare were highly prized since she and Anthony had been quarantined at Lucinda Barrington's abode, but it took only a moment to realize these lines were of more recent advent. While Nan continued with her hair, Ginny read the beautiful verses, then read them again. And again.

> *If ever an Angel mine eyes did behold*
> *With snowy white wings and a halo of gold*
> *Or if there a mermaid should somewhere be found*
> *Whose voice flowed like honey, whose hair bathed the ground*
> *Or should there a Siren's sweet song fill the air*
> *Or spied I a rainbow, you'd not find me there*
> *For these make little impression on me*
> *All pale in the face of the beauty in thee.*
>
> *Oh, I could adventure upon the high seas*
> *And sail the world over however I pleased*
> *Or I could climb mountains, ford river and stream*
> *In search of my destiny, chasing a dream.*
> *Yea, many's the wonder I'm yearning to see*
> *And places aplenty my heart longs to be*
> *Though countless and sundry the things I could do*
> *My soul lies content simply being with you.*
>
> *~Jusqu'a ce soir, A.*

Surely Anthony had penned the beautiful verses himself. Her heart, suffused with joy, felt lighter than it had since the night he had asked her to be his wife.

"Oh, them's just lovely words, aren't they?" Nan said in a breathless voice as she read over Ginny's shoulder. Nan had admired Sir Anthony from the moment she had met him years before, and the fact that Ginny was to marry him was her dearest wish. For that reason Ginny hadn't revealed to Nan any of the doubts she was feeling with regard to her ultimate suitability as the future Duchess of Marcross.

" 'Jusku see sour.' What does that mean, Miss?"

"It means 'until tonight,' " Ginny answered, "and that he will be in attendance at one or more of the parties I shall be attending, as well. I do hope it is the soiree. There is no dancing at a rout, and I so want to tell him how very much I cherish his poem."

"Why ever can't you tell him at the rout? What is the difference between it and a sour-ay, anyway? They both sound frenchy to me," Nan said, wrinkling her nose.

"Routs are rather taxing," Ginny replied, carefully folding up the poem and placing it in the drawer of her dressing table. "If, during the long wait in the queue of carriages, one doesn't give up the idea of ever gaining entrance to the house, one is obliged to push one's way up the staircase, wishing all the while she had never come, only to be hastened through the house by the press of people at one's back, down the hall, and on down the stairs for the interminable wait for one's carriage to reappear. And all this for the chance to bid good evening to your host and hostess and have a cordial of ratafia, if one should be so lucky. Lord Crenshaw could be a mere foot or two away, and I would never get near him."

"If you ask me, miss, those routs sound about as painful as gittin' burned with the curling tongs! You couldn't git me near one of those for a thousand pound! Why doesn't Sir Anthony take you up in his own carriage?"

"It is to be 'Lord Crenshaw' for the time being, Nan," Ginny chastised. "At least until the duke dies, and then it will be 'Your Grace.' " The very words made Ginny feel a bit sick to her stomach. "As for why he is to meet us rather than attend us, well, it is a rather difficult situation. It will be his first public appearance since the death of his cousin. It wasn't seemly to announce our betrothal on the heels of such a tragedy, and I daresay Lord Crenshaw hasn't had time to send notice to the papers."

Yet he had made time to write her that lovely bit of poetry. As much as she cherished his words of love, she felt a shadow of doubt. How long would it take to dash off a short note, sand it, fold it, and apply his seal? Surely not nearly as long as it must have taken to write the poem. Ginny pushed the unworthy thought from her mind and tried to recapture the thread of conversation.

"You should jist tell that ol' windbag never no mind about the routs," Nan urged. "And you only want to go to the sour-ay!"

"If by 'old windbag' you mean Grandaunt Regina," Ginny reprimanded, "would that it were so simple." Ginny sighed. There would be many routs to attend once she became a duchess and many more at which she would stand as hostess, pinned in the gimlet glare of her exacting mother-in-law. It was imperative she learn all she could as to how these things were done.

As Nan tied the tapes at the back of her gown, Ginny scrutinized its suitability in the pier glass. It was white, as were all the evening gowns worn by the young ladies in their *débutante* season. Before her fateful return to the country, Ginny had finally been presented to the Queen, as well, yet she was no young miss just out of the schoolroom, and she loathed that she wouldn't be allowed to wear colors for evening until after her wedding day.

As a means to stave off ennui, this ensemble was as different from her wedding gown as possible. Instead of fine-as-silk muslin, it was satin. Instead of a moderate neckline, it was quite low. Instead of rows of pin-tucks and embroidered flowers, the waist was excessively high, leaving very little bodice at all to hold up the puffed sleeves trimmed with silver-spangled lace. Her gowns for later in the season would make more allowances for the heat, but being as it was still May, the white velvet ribbon that separated the bodice from the skirt and the yards and yards of ruched velvet at the hem did not look terribly out of place. It was all a bit too fussy for Ginny, but she owned that Grandaunt had impeccable taste and knew what would be most appropriate for a young lady betrothed to a future duke.

However, when it was finally time to depart, it was a bit of an art to get the new gown all gathered up into the carriage, being as it was fuller around the hem than most and the satin quite stiff.

"Don't fret about it, my dear," Grandaunt insisted. "In my day it was necessary to kneel in the carriage so one's headdress wasn't knocked from your head, balanced as they were on those monstrously high wigs. And the skirts! They were a hundred times more voluminous than yours and contained enormous hoops. It's a wonder they remained intact long enough to arrive anywhere. More often than not, we wore each gown but the once, so it did not signify."

Ginny, whose father had felt it scandalous to have a new gown made up but once a season, feared she would never grow accustomed to a life of privilege. The gown in which she was clad would doubtless feed a crofter's entire family for a month or more. Once she was Duchess of Marcross, she would find a way to help those less fortunate. She would start by wearing each and every gown at least twice. She hoped Anthony would not think it made her look a dowd.

"Now then, Ginerva, we must first stop at the Worthingtons' rout. Thomasina will never forgive me if I miss her do. Then it will be the Radcliffs' rout, and the soiree last, so you might dance as long as you wish."

"Oh, I *am* glad! I so hoped to save the Hadleys and the dancing for last!"

"Yes, well, I feel I was a bit hasty in sending Anthony off in the middle of a contretemps, but I see that you are in better spirits now." Grandaunt patted Ginny on the knee. "Hopefully

Miss Delacourt Has Her Day 37

you will have a chance to clear things up a bit, though, if I am not wrong, I believe you received a missive from him. Would I be too much of a nosy one to ask what he wrote?"

Grandaunt was never wrong, even when she was. What's more, Ginny had never known her to care one jot for whether or not she was intruding on one's privacy. Clearly she was giving Ginny a wide berth, and Ginny feared it meant that her grandaunt was feeling more than a little anxiety. Ginny drew a deep breath and chose her words carefully.

"Yes, he wrote to say he would be attending one of the do's we go to tonight, but I can't be sure which one."

"Never you fear! I took it upon myself to dispatch my own note. He will be at the soiree, and you shall have your dance."

"Grandaunt, you are so kind!" Ginny wondered what accounted for it. Grandaunt was not above high-handed meddling—in fact, she rather wallowed in it—but it was not like her to be so thoughtful in her methods. Yet, Ginny owned, Grandaunt above all else wished for her grandson's happiness and would stop at nothing to achieve it, apparently even if it meant stooping to kindness. Ginny prayed she was still deemed essential to Anthony's happiness in Grandaunt's mind. After reading Anthony's poem, she knew she was in his.

The Radcliff rout was a sight better than the Worthingtons' hot and hasty affair, but only because Anthony thought he caught a glimpse of the back of Ginny's head as she scurried through the crush of people intent on bowing and scraping to the Marquis of Radcliff and his marchioness. How could he have ever enjoyed such affairs designed for nothing better than to see and be seen? And why hadn't Grandmama had the grace to share with him which party she would be attending tonight rather than listing them all? Surely she didn't mean to drag poor Ginny to all three. But if not, which ones? There was nothing for it but to hasten through the routs and hope he would be in the Hadleys' home long enough to at least encounter Ginny.

He would much rather dance with her, truth be told, but he would take anything, must have *some*thing, even if just an eyeful, to get him through the night. To his chagrin, a perhaps-yes, perhaps-no viewing of the back of her head did nothing to quench his thirst for the sight of her.

Pushing through the throng, sidestepping a fallen glass of port here and a wad of wayward snuff there, he raced through the house and to the stairs in record time. Never mind that he had practically snubbed the marquis and his lady wife once he found himself close enough to greet them. They would no doubt take it to be on account of his suddenly heightened status. Hadn't the vile Thomas Barron looked down his lofty nose at the world when he unexpectedly became Marquis of Radcliff, and for less reason? In the case of the future Duke of Marcross, only love would be allowed to break down the door of what he deemed polite, and he feared love was on its way to a rout he had already attended.

Racing out into the street, he barked his name to the porter and scanned the crowds waiting for their carriages as well as those being disgorged from theirs. It was utter confusion and madness, but one person seemed to notice none of it as she moved toward him with single-minded purpose. Lady Derby.

Was it merely his imagination, or were the crowds, like the Red Sea, parting in anticipation of her passage directly to where he stood? And were the guests all watching him, their faces the very picture of so many gasping fish that find they have suddenly landed on dry ground? Anthony knew he would be waiting an eternity for his carriage to be brought 'round and would have no other option than to speak to her. The thought of diving into the swarms of people and pelting down the street like a bedlamite occurred to him, but Rebecca was upon him before he had a chance to so much as turn his head.

"Why, Tony!" Lady Derby purred, slipping her arm through his and tucking it against her side. "I had thought you would be with that child bride of yours."

"She is *not* my bride. That is to say, she is not a *child*." Drat his mother, for surely it was she who had so fully informed Lady Derby of what his uncle insisted be a secret. He hadn't the chance to talk with Ginny about delaying the announcement in the papers for a few more days until he could think of a way to make everyone happy about his decision to wed, but it was a small problem compared to Lady Derby's skill in twisting everything, including his tongue, into knots.

"What she is, is not *here*," Lady Derby said with a wide-eyed look that took in the persons standing near and far. "Did her governess not think it prudent to let her out tonight?" she asked, biting her lip in feigned woe.

"Lady Derby, need I remind you that when you received your first offer of marriage, you were still in short skirts?"

"Oh, Tony, you remembered!" she said, rapping him on the arm with her fan. "It seems you had a penchant for young maidens even then."

Fiend seize her, she had made his reprimand sound like flirtation! "And how could you forget," he said as loudly as he dared for the benefit of the madding crowd, "that your first offer of marriage was from Thomas, Lord Radcliff?" He added for her ears only, "Hadn't you better hurry inside? The marchioness is looking a bit bilious. You never know when her husband's offer of marriage to you might be renewed." And with a bow that required she let go of his arm, he stepped between two waiting carriages and melted into the night.

Running up the street, he happily came across his own carriage and jumped inside. With any luck, he would be to the soiree before Ginny had left or, better yet, before she arrived. He would need a moment to find a mirror and repair his appearance. Quickly, he straightened his cuffs and smoothed his dark locks with the little silver comb he carried in his pocket. His cravat, however, would have to wait until he could see what he was doing. He did not, to his sorrow, have his valet's gift for tying one, but allowing Conti to trot along behind him as he went from one entertainment to the next would only make Anthony an object of fun.

Anthony could see that the Hadleys' soiree was in full swing when he arrived. After checking his cravat in the hall mirror, he scanned the room for Ginny. Mrs. Hadley, Grandmama's bosom friend since childhood, had not attracted the title and monies her ancestry warranted. As a result, the house was small and lacked a ballroom. Furniture in the main sitting room had been pushed aside and the carpets rolled up to allow for the dancing, lending the proceedings an exceptionally cozy feel. The atmosphere was such that a few quiet minutes alone with Ginny in a corner somewhere would not seem overly amiss. He knew he should discuss the subject of his conversation with his uncle, but above all else he wished to hear her thoughts and feelings with regard to his poem. It looked, however, as if he would have to wait, as Ginny was neither among the dancers nor any of the observers.

He wandered into the dining room, where platters of food and drink had been laid out for supper, but she was absent from there, as well. He knew he had a better chance of locating his grandmama despite her lack of height, so voluminous became her voice after a few cordials of canary, but he heard nothing that would lead him to believe she and Ginny had arrived.

"Oh, Lord Crenshaw!" came a voice at his shoulder. "Might I trouble you for a moment?"

Anthony turned around and came face to face with Mrs. Hadley. He had forgotten she was so tall that one was tempted to measure her years in inches—a sad fact that no doubt contributed to her status as a mere Mrs., her father, the viscount, and large dowry notwithstanding. One did hope for tall sons but doubtless wished for a more abbreviated wife to get them by.

"Mrs. Hadley, how grateful I am to have received an invitation. It has been too long since I have been within the portals of your lovely home."

Mrs. Hadley let forth a string of titters. Anthony had long suspected the gruesome noises to be laughter, but he could never be quite sure, as they punctuated every utterance from him or any other, no matter the subject or degree of levity. Doubtless this had been another blow against her chances of making a fine match.

"Lord Crenshaw, how sad we were to learn of your cousin's death! I see you wear your black armband," she remarked.

It was the only condolence followed by hysterical laughter he had ever received. The utter ridiculousness of the situation almost undid him, but he quickly sobered when Mrs. Hadley drew a nearby girl to her side with an arm about her waist. She was of a height with Mrs. Hadley and was surely some variety of relative. Just which variation, he was sure to learn.

"In light of your renewed status, you must be on a sharp lookout for a bride. Oh, and look whom I have here! This is my lovely granddaughter," Mrs. Hadley said, upon which both she and her youthful doppelgänger burst into a series of titters and strangled guffaws.

Anthony wondered how his grandmama had put herself through the agony of developing such a long-lasting attachment with Mrs. Hadley. Worse, he began to suspect he was expected to make a similar one with her granddaughter. With the studied grace of years of practice he refrained from sighing aloud. "Might I have the pleasure of being introduced?"

"But of course, my lord, of course! May I introduce Miss Burton, Hepzibah, better known as Kazzy? So daft how these names go, is it not? Hepzibah, Heppy, Hezzy, Kezzy, Kazzy! One never knows what someone might end up being called, do they?"

"No, indeed," Anthony replied, and this time he allowed himself a sigh, as it would surely go unheard and unnoticed in the gale of titters that followed. With an inward wince, he resigned himself to the fate of an eligible lord of nobility, one bound to be replete with doting mothers and grandmothers wishful to force the acquaintance of their kin upon his person. It was an unenviable state but one he hoped to endure until his attachment to Ginny would become public knowledge. Until then he knew he could not do his hostess the dishonor of refusing to dance with any number of eligible young ladies in attendance.

"Miss Burton, might I have the honor for the next set?"

He took the inevitable gasps and titters to be a "yes" and, taking her by the hand, led her back into the parlor.

The moment he stepped foot into the room, his head turned, almost of its own accord, to a far corner. There stood Ginny in a white gown, looking just as he had pictured her on their wedding day. When her gaze met his, and that slow blush he so adored stole along her cheeks, he felt as if the wind had been knocked out if him. Gad, she was beautiful! He wanted nothing more than to go to her, but he had a duty to perform, and he was being tugged out into the dancing. It wasn't until he turned to face his partner that he learned that the one now holding his hand was none other than Lady Derby.

Chapter Five

From her place in the corner, Ginny watched the proceedings with interest. "Why, that woman pushed aside that poor girl!" she gasped. "I believe she is crying!"

"No, it is but laughter," Grandaunt said with a grimace. "But that is neither here nor there. Kazzy is kin to my dear Mrs. Hadley, and 'that woman' is none other than Lady Derby. She was never one to sit by and watch while others, er, danced." She pursed her lips in a show of disapproval. "I wonder what she has planned for my grandson and how very put out she will be once she gets a glimpse of you."

Ginny felt a rush of affection for her grandaunt but could not agree. "I can only assume she will find me no threat whatsoever." She regarded Lady Derby closely. With her thick hair arranged in a wondrously intricate style atop her head, her dark, flashing eyes, her flawless skin and pleasingly curved figure, she was easily the most beautiful woman in the room. Her title and fortune were more closely aligned with Anthony's than those of any other woman in the room, as well.

Ginny narrowed her gaze at Anthony and Lady Derby as they danced and conversed and even smiled into each other's eyes, then turned to her grandaunt. "I think I shall go look for something to drink in the supper room." She sailed away without another glance but knew Anthony watched her go. She could feel his gaze hot on her back and suspected Lady Derby might be as interested in every detail of her person as Ginny was in hers.

She raised her chin just a fraction. After all, a duchess did not let her knees go out from under her when faced with the mere hint of trouble. Nevertheless, she found a chair to sink into the moment she was beyond Lady Derby's scope and burst into tears. She was grateful Grandaunt had stayed behind and would never know how she fell so completely to pieces. It would not do for anyone to see her otherwise but in total possession of her emotions. A duchess did not cry in public. Perhaps not even in private. She tried to imagine her grandaunt undone by tears and could not.

The clapping and stamping of the contra dance going on in the next room came to a halt before Ginny could stem the flow of tears. She had just stood and stepped to the sideboard to ladle out a cup of punch when she heard a much-loved voice from the doorway.

"Allow me," Anthony said. Before she could utter a word, he had stepped to her side, poured the punch, taken her hand in his, and placed the cup gently in her grasp. "I am told the next set is to be a waltz, and I have it on very good authority you are a dab hand at waltzing. Will you so honor me, Miss Delacourt?"

Ginny felt the blush rise in her face and hastily looked around the room to determine if any of the people milling about had noticed their exchange. She knew their betrothal had not yet been announced, even if she did not know the reason why, and she felt the importance of being discreet. However, there could be nothing exceptionable with regard to their dancing together. It was why she had come.

"My lord, I should be delighted." Abandoning the cup of punch after only one sip, she put her hand in his and allowed herself to be led to the queue of couples lining up to dance. She tried not to think of how she would be thoroughly inspected in just the same way she had Lady Derby—indeed,

Miss Delacourt Has Her Day

the way every woman Anthony partnered that night would be—but it was to no avail. Her mouth went suddenly dry, and her legs once again threatened to give out beneath her.

"Come, Miss Delacourt," Anthony said. "I'm not going to eat you!" Then, soft and low, so no one but she could hear, he added, "I must confess, when I saw you first tonight, it was all I could do to keep from rushing to your side and soundly kissing you."

"Anthony!" she hissed. "Have a care. Everyone will see my blushes and wonder what you are saying to cause them."

His reply was lost, for just then a chord was struck, and the waltzing began. "I'm sorry, you were saying?" She dared to glance up and was bathed in the brilliance of his smile, one she hadn't seen but a handful of times in all the days she had known him. The real him.

"I said, let them see your blushes!" he replied with a squeeze of her hand in his. "They will only think how splendid you look in them."

"You wicked man," she said in a playful air, one totally at odds with the glow of gratitude she felt, bathed in the warmth of his approval. "Why, they shall have much opportunity to decide how I look in them now!" She glanced away to gain some composure—a hopeless endeavor, considering the heat of his hand at her waist and the proximity of his lips to her own.

"Now that I have you somewhat to myself, pray tell what you thought of my poem."

Ginny glanced up at him in surprise. How could she have forgotten? She saw a spark of something bordering on uncertainty in his eyes and owned she was surprised by that, as well. "I thought it perfectly glorious! And not only because it was written with myself in mind."

"Oh?" He waggled his eyebrows at her. "Are you so sure of yourself? It is rather presumptuous, is it not?"

"Do go on, Lord Crenshaw," Ginny said with a fond smile. "I am persuaded the entire room, including Lady Derby, are all agog to know what is causing this uncharacteristic liveliness of expression in your face."

He looked away. "Let us not speak of Lady Derby. Instead I shall dwell on your words of admiration for my freshman attempt at Shakespeare-like éclat."

Ginny knew it her most heartfelt desire to admire him excessively in every way, but she could hardly say so. "I have many more such words of praise, but first I believe we must, at the very least, sanction our attachment with a betrothal." Ginny paused and bit her lip. She did not wish to be seen as a tiresome faultfinder and so sought to temper her words. "If I heard aright, there was some talk of the duke and his reaction to news of our betrothal rising above the babble of my weeping this afternoon. You must think me the most abominable blubberer. When I am a duchess, I promise I shall never weep."

"When you are duchess, you shall do as you very well please!" he admonished her with a frown.

Ginny gasped. "You did not glare so at Lady Derby when you danced with her. Indeed, you were smiling."

Anthony smiled. "Yes, I was, just as I am now, but I was not in the least happy."

"As you are now unhappy?" she asked with an arched eyebrow. "And I suppose I am to admire you for your talent for speaking while displaying every one of your teeth? Might you lessen your grimace a trifle in order to answer my question with regard to the duke?" It would be senseless in the extreme to add another query on top of that, one having to do with why he had scolded her and yet another having to do with whether or not he had ever known a duchess to cry.

He had the grace to look a bit discomfited by her words; then he pulled her tightly against his chest, preventing her a view of his face. "As for the duke, I had meant to speak with you upon that very subject when I called this afternoon."

Ginny, her ear pressed to his cravat, which smelled of shaving cream, fresh linen, and something warm and heady and unique to him, could feel his words rumbling in his chest as much as hear them. "I only wish my time had not been so wholly taken up by the Averys," she replied, whereupon he bent his head to hers as if to better perceive her words.

Perhaps it was the deft ease with which he moved, as if there were no constraints between them, or perhaps it was how comfortable he seemed with his head poised so close to hers, but it was a particularly intimate gesture, too intimate for a pair who did not wish to give the impression they had spent much time in each other's company. She shivered, both with delight and apprehension.

"Mayhap our conversation is better left until we are no longer dancing. People are beginning to take notice." Lady Derby, in particular, was staring at them over the shoulder of her dancing partner at every opportunity, and it was clear from the glint in her eyes that she did not like what she saw. The way Anthony suddenly stiffened made Ginny think perhaps he had noticed, as well.

"Forgive me, Ginny, but I feel it would be best if I depart when this dance is over," he said very low but loudly enough for her to hear without his head being but a hairbreadth away. "Might we continue this conversation tomorrow? Say, in the morning? But only if you are fully recovered from your late evening of dancing with every man in the room, as surely you shall, my darling girl."

Ginny nodded when she would have preferred to throw herself into his arms and beg him to stay, to dance every dance with her. What use did she have for any other man in the room but he? Besides, there was Lady Derby with whom to be reckoned. She, no doubt, would have something unpleasant to say as soon as Ginny was no longer safe in his arms.

As it was, she hadn't even that long to wait.

"Why, this must be the country mouse to whom you have given your heart!" Lady Derby quipped the moment the music had ceased. She was still clasped in the arms of her dancing partner, whose goggle-eyed look implied he was as discommoded by her pronouncement as if he were the intended target of her malice.

"Er, pardon me, Lady Derby," the man murmured, and he jerked his hands from her as if from a scorching fire. "I will just see about a glass of, of, of . . ."

And then he was gone, vanishing through the crowd of dancers turned statues. Very attentive statues, Ginny could not help but notice.

She stole a glance at Anthony from the corner of her eye. She could see he was angry and waited with bated breath to see which version of himself would make an appearance: the polite yet sometimes cruel Sir Anthony-of-the-mask she once knew, or the true-speaking man behind the mask she had come to love.

"Lady Derby, might I have the pleasure of introducing Miss Delacourt, lately of Bedfordshire, and my affianced bride?"

Ginny heard Grandaunt Regina's gasp of disapproval above the instant chatter that rose like the crackle of fire in a field of stubble. It seemed she was as anxious to keep the engagement a secret as was her son, the duke. The thought gave Ginny no comfort. Meanwhile, the glares of disapprobation from many a mother intent on one day seeing her daughter as Duchess of Marcross were unsettling in the extreme.

"Anthony," she said in as small a voice as possible, "I think we should leave."

"I wouldn't hear of it!" cried Lady Derby, who, it would seem, was as sharp in her hearing as in her observations. "Why, it would behoove you to stay and enjoy yourself. I daresay we might even persuade one or two gentlemen to stand up with you for a dance while you glean from present company just how things are done in London. No doubt your time shut up in the country has not availed you of the ways of Society."

Ginny opened her mouth to give vent to the blistering reply on her tongue, but Lady Derby had so accurately fingered each of Ginny's doubts, her lungs were frozen in anxious fear. It was just as well. If she had spoken, she would certainly have made matters far worse. As it was, the thought of Lady Derby and Anthony's mother chatting about this disastrous turn of events over tea and biscuits made her long for the power to sink through the floor.

Anthony gave her a look of puzzled concern before stepping forward and putting out an arm as if to shield her from the company at large. "It's a pity, Lady Derby, that your late husband's country seat is in Derbyshire. Why, that's as near to Wales as could be—a practical wilderness! You have no doubt forgotten our ways here in town. I believe it has always been considered beyond the pale to insult a lady, whether the insult is delivered by a lady or not."

Grandaunt's gasp was much louder this time. Ginny thought perhaps she had gasped, as well, but couldn't be sure, as all sound was swallowed up in the roar of stampeding guests making a horrified dash for the refreshment parlor. Only Lady Derby seemed utterly unaffected by Anthony's defense. Her smile was pleasant, her alabaster skin as unblemished by emotion as ever, her stance perfectly poised and gracious. In short, she behaved exactly as a duchess should behave in the face of hideous scandal. Ginny thought she had never felt more naïve, ignorant, nor decidedly unlike a duchess than she did at that moment.

When Anthony took her tenderly by the arm to be fussed over by Grandaunt, she felt defeated. When he ignored Lady Derby's unnerving proximity and whispered into Ginny's ear, "It doesn't matter—all will be well," she felt miserable. When he turned to give her one last glance before finding his hostess and begging her pardon for departing so soon, she felt completely abandoned. He had done everything an attentive and loving future husband should. So why did she feel so betrayed?

Numb with the prospect of impending doom, Ginny allowed herself to be wrapped up in her cloak, prodded down the stairs, out the door, and into the carriage without a word passing her lips. There was nothing to say, nothing to think of but her inapprehensible plight. For the first time in her life, she wished she had a mask to hide behind, a mask that hid her less-than-admirable thoughts and actions, one that prompted her to always say and do what was proper. It was ironic that she, who had never cared for the shallow ways of Society, should be teeming with desire to be admitted into their ranks. How laughably implausible! Had she allowed herself to occupy so untenable a position that she actually feared being ruined in the eyes of Society?

"Oh, Grandaunt Regina!" she said, daring to lay her head on the duchess' shoulder in the confines of the ink-dark carriage. "What a woman won't do for love!"

"Yes, my dear," said the duchess with an uncharacteristic pat to Ginny's cheek. "Indeed!"

Chapter Six

"Everything always looks better in the morning." Those had been Grandaunt's last words to Ginny after seeing her tucked snugly into bed and blowing out the candles with her very own regal lips. Now, in the morning light, its rays reflected in the silky counterpane spread across her bed, Ginny thought perhaps Grandaunt was right. Surely the situation was not as bad as she'd feared last night. In fact, now that their engagement had been made somewhat public, perhaps Anthony would be willing to choose a date for their wedding.

Remembering he had promised to arrive early to discuss their impending marriage, she pushed aside her niggling doubts about the duke's disapproval and hurried through her morning ablutions in hopes Anthony planned to join her and Grandaunt in time for breakfast. Looking around, she noticed it was earlier than she supposed; Nan had not appeared to help her dress, and the maid hadn't yet been in to light the fires.

Shivering, she pulled her warmest dress from the clothespress, a linsey-woolsey in soft gray she hadn't worn since winter. It was a favorite, as it was a bit too long, leaving plenty of skirt in which to wrap her bare feet when she curled up by the fire with a book. She had forgotten the hem was both a bit stretched out and falling down as a result of the abuse she had given it, but since it was the easiest of her gowns to don herself, she decided it was her quickest option. The quicker the better. She had waited long enough to learn exactly what it was the duke had had to say about Anthony's attachment to her, and there were the events of last night to mull over, as well. Mostly she wanted to sit by his side and merely look at him, hear his voice, breathe his scent, and wait for the kiss he always managed to arrange even while under Grandaunt's watchful eye.

Sighing, she began to hunt for shoes. Her dancing slippers were the closest to hand, but she rejected them for the blue kid ones she wore about the house. After donning them, there was nothing left to do but tie a ribbon around her unruly curls. It was a green one that clashed with everything but her eyes, but no matter; she knew Anthony would not think it too loud against the more demure coloring of her gown.

Finally she was dressed and with not a moment to lose. She could hear the opening and closing of the front door and the murmur of voices raised in greeting as she hurried down the hall. Taking the stairs at a brisk pace, she caught her toe in the damaged hem of her skirt and tumbled nearly the entire way down to land in an undignified heap at the bottom. The picture she presented when she had righted herself was only slightly less undignified. Her hem torn, her hair falling down with the ribbon trailing down her back, and one blue kid slipper in her hand, she looked up to bid good morning to her guest, only to be greeted with a loud "Harrumph!" from her future mother-in-law.

"Oh! Lady Crenshaw. I had not expected it to be you." Ginny thrust the hand holding the shoe behind her and attempted to get it reunited with her foot without anyone the wiser. "That is to say, I had not expected you! At least, not so early in the morning." *Oh, dear!* She was making mice feet of the whole affair, and just when she most needed to be all that was irreproachable.

"You were doubtless expecting my son," Lady Crenshaw announced as she sailed down the hall to the parlor without the aid of the butler, who had wisely decamped. "However, after the debacle of last night, he has once again been summoned to the duke's side."

Ginny, feeling her boat was well and truly sunk, followed sedately along behind. In a no doubt fruitless bid at decorum, she pulled the green ribbon from her hair and left it on the hall table as she passed. Anthony, should he ever arrive, would have to admire the gray-green of her eyes without it.

"Well!" Lady Crenshaw exclaimed upon pushing open the door and glancing around the parlor, "I can see she has done nothing to improve this room since last I was here." She sat gingerly on the edge of the sofa, almost as if its being a few years past the crack of fashion were contagious. "I generously informed her how this gold brocade would never do, but she isn't one who cherishes the opinions of others, do you not agree?"

Ginny most assuredly did. She felt Anthony's mother was cut from the same bolt of cloth as Grandaunt but knew it would not help her case to open her budget on the subject.

"Lady Crenshaw, I am so surprised, ah, honored at your visit. Have you breakfasted?" Ginny would be shocked to learn that she had. In London, no one who was anyone rose much before noon during the season, Grandaunt included, and it was still early for even those who were meant to wait on their betters.

"No, I have not, and I lay the fault entirely in your dish!" Lady Crenshaw retorted. "I haven't had a morsel or slept a wink since I had news from certain persons about the scandal you put into motion last night."

Ginny swallowed a hot retort of her own, but her empty stomach was having none of it. "I am sorry to hear you have been so ill. Perhaps the fault would be better assigned to those persons who so thoughtlessly carried this exaggerated news to you," she suggested as she rang the bell for refreshments to be served.

Lady Crenshaw sat back and raised her eyebrows in scorn.

"I had the news of Lady Derby herself, last night at the Seftons' rout. I have no reason to believe she spoke an untrue word. Her description of you making eyes at my son, dancing all night with him, and causing a literal scandal on the dance floor is exactly the kind of behavior I would have expected of one such as you!"

Ginny was too angry to formulate a reply to any but one of the charges. "We had but one dance. We were only under Mrs. Hadley's roof together for a matter of minutes. Surely not even Lady Derby could construe that to mean we were together all night. I—"

"Tut-tut!" Lady Crenshaw interrupted. "Why, you make it sound as if Lady Derby is stirring up trouble merely to make things difficult!"

Ginny knew the case to be exactly that but feared any reply she made would only further ruin any chance she had at pleasing Lady Crenshaw. She was momentarily saved by the arrival of the tea tray and a cart bearing breakfast food. Sadly, Ginny had lost her appetite and could only watch as Lady Crenshaw loaded her plate with buttered toast, bacon, scones, and clotted cream.

"You realize what this means," Lady Derby said, frowning around a mouthful of food.

"I'm sorry, I do not. Is the cream soured?" Ginny asked. "I will ring for Garner to take it away at once."

"It is not the cream that is in danger of souring, Miss Delacourt," Lady Crenshaw said with a meaningful stare.

Ginny quickly scanned the food cart for other perishables. "Oh, dear. Do you mean to say the butter has gone bad?"

"I can see that I shall have to say this straight out," Lady Crenshaw said with a heavy sigh. "My son is to be the next Duke of Marcross. Whatever you think of such, please know that Lord Crenshaw holds his future title in high regard and fully understands the responsibility he has for the family name and honor. When he formed his . . . attachment for you," Lady Crenshaw said with a shudder, "you must own that it was before he knew what his future held in store."

"I am sure neither of us dreamed this would be our lot, Lady Crenshaw, but I can assure you that I will do my best to honor my title as the future duchess."

Lady Crenshaw emitted a rueful little laugh and put aside her plate. "You? Duchess? Miss Delacourt, do you not perceive the importance of his making a brilliant marriage?"

Ginny formulated her reply with care. "Yes, I do, but I am persuaded you discount the importance your son places on true affection for his chosen wife."

"Poof! Love," Lady Crenshaw said with a wave of her hand. "If only you knew how little that means once the passion subsides. The look he has in his eyes when he speaks of you is no different than the sparkle he bore when he was courting Lady Derby!"

Ginny, her stomach roiling with apprehension, cast about for the proper duchesslike response to such hurtful words but found there was none.

"He can fall in love with a girl who is a suitable match as well as one who is, well... *not*," Lady Crenshaw continued with a sickly sweet smile, then leaned toward Ginny over her cup and saucer as if to keep her words from the wrong ears. "If you truly love Anthony, you will release my son in order to save him the scandal of breaking the engagement himself. Surely you can understand that," she said with a sweeping glance of Ginny's person, "even if you are no better than a guttersnipe."

Ginny opened her mouth to reply but was shocked when the voice of her Grandaunt rang loud and clear. "That will be enough out of you, Deborah! Ginerva is the granddaughter of my own brother, and he was a Wembley!"

Lady Crenshaw rose to her feet in a huff. "And I suppose the Wembley name is better than ours."

"It is good enough. However, if bearing a noble name gives

you free rein to behave like a rag-mannered fool, my Ginny shall be glad to be free of it!"

"Well, I never! I suppose I should thank you for that! In point of fact, I shall waste no time in getting word to Anthony that the engagement is at *point non plus!*" Lady Crenshaw cried as she hastened from the room.

Grandaunt waited until the sound of her daughter-in-law's ranting went down the stairs and out the front door before she turned to Ginny, her expression inscrutable. "I believe I warned you to let me handle Lady Crenshaw. Now, go and change your clothes. You look a fright. I expect my grandson will be calling at any moment, and we wouldn't want him to have reason to think you a guttersnipe, as well." Then she, too, quit the room.

Ginny longed to throw something, anything, but it was the one habit of hers Anthony had expressly forbidden. In every other way, for every other virtue and vice, he loved her just as she was. She would not have him enter the room to witness her failure to change the one thing about herself he objected to when there was so much about her that was objectionable.

However, she did not change her gown or her shoes or tidy her hair. She went down to the kitchen and out the door to the small walled garden and took up a bench in the morning sun to wait, knowing he would eventually find her. Wherever she was, wherever she might go, he would never fail to find her.

Why the devil could he not find her? He had searched the breakfast room, the morning room, the parlor, and even Grandmama's study. He was about to start opening bedchamber doors willy-nilly, but was stopped in his tracks by the sight of a green ribbon on the hall table. It was his favorite color for Ginny to wear, much greener than her eyes but just the thing to coax the emerald sparkle out of her mostly gray orbs. Pocketing the ribbon, he resolved to buy her yards and yards of the stuff—if only he could find her!

He headed up the stairs to the third floor and opened the first door he came to. The room that lay beyond was furnished in dark wood, and blue velvet hangings adorned the bed. He realized with a start that it was the room he had been given for his use on those few occasions he had stayed with Grandmama since she had taken up residence at Wembley House after his grandfather's death. Only once had he stayed overnight when Ginny had also been in London, yet he had no solid memory of her at that time. It seemed strange that she had slept in a room just down the hall, had sat at breakfast across the table from him, and he, all the while, was without the slightest inkling of how deeply in love with her he would one day be.

True, at the time, he and Ginny had moved in very different circles. She, preferring books and flowers to the company of Society, had all but given up moving around in her delegated circle, while he had simply moved around and around in his, getting nowhere at all whatsoever.

He drifted to the window. There must have been times when she was hiding out in the garden, wishing him at Jericho, while he was in the house busy with his own activities, too intent on nursing the paltry wound Lady Derby's betrayal had done to his pride to notice how Ginny had blossomed into a beautiful, intelligent woman. It had happened right before his very eyes, but he never saw it until one fateful day a fortnight—and a lifetime—ago.

Suddenly he saw her sunning herself on a bench in the garden, her feet curled up in the hem of her gown. Her hair, he noticed, was lacking adornment of any kind and hung down about her shoulders in scandalous disarray. She was gazing off into the distance, an air of patient waiting stamped upon her features. She looked for all the world like something out of a fairy tale, one in which the prince has been long delayed with the slaying of dragons while the beautiful and virtuous milkmaid remains steadfast and faithful that he will save the day and return to her side.

If only he hadn't been so caught up in the ways of Society, he might have come to her much sooner.

She looked up then and saw him. The smile that lit her face made his breath catch in his throat. He was torn between standing there to drink in that smile forever and climbing out the window to take her instantly into his arms.

"We are on the third floor, you buffle-headed fool!"

Anthony whirled to face the door. "Grandmama! How did . . ."

"You talk to yourself. Out loud. I daresay your valet has mentioned it to you once or twice. He finds it disconcerting in the extreme, but it has its advantages," she said with a nod at the window. "Now, go and tell her what you have come to say, but use the stairs! I won't have you breaking your head open on my property. I would much prefer you make that your mother's problem, should push come to shove."

Anthony felt an icy finger make its way down the length of his spine. "My mother? Has she been here already?"

"At the crack of dawn, riding her broomstick."

Anthony groaned. "That is all that is needed! How did Ginny fare? Is she terribly upset?"

"She didn't throw anything, if that is what you are wondering." She sighed and sank onto the bed, looking suddenly every day of her age. "Anthony, matters are much worse than the trouble stirred up by Lady Derby, and I fear it is all my fault."

Anthony was alarmed by his grandmother's tone. He had never seen her like this, tired and vulnerable, old, even. He sat next to her and put an arm about her shoulders. "Whatever it is that has happened, dearest, we shall all come about."

"Oh, my boy, my precious boy, I fear not!" she cried, her lips trembling.

"Grandmama, you are crying!"

"Impossible!" she said, pushing him away. "Now, just . . . you must go to her, Anthony. Comfort her as an old lady cannot."

Miss Delacourt Has Her Day 59

He hesitated to leave Grandmama in such a state, but the way he was being swatted and pushed toward the door left him in little doubt of her wishes. As he dreaded outlining to her the details of his conversation with his uncle, the duke, only an hour previous, he was more than a bit relieved to get away and decided he would write to her the odious news in a note to be delivered via the post as soon as the moment presented itself. No doubt his uncle would do so, as well.

He went downstairs and out toward the tiny garden with an ever-increasing feeling of dread. First his uncle the duke had turned on him, then his mother, and now Grandmama. What sort of family had he invited Ginny to join? If she were wise, she would run screaming into the wilderness before becoming a Crenshaw. Instead, she was waiting where he had last seen her, glowing in a patch of sunshine.

"I was beginning to think I was wrong, that you would never find me," she said with a misty smile.

Dropping to the bench beside her, he gathered her into his arms. "My poor girl! Has it been as bad as all that?"

Ginny gave a watery chuckle and leaned back out of his embrace. "Your grandmama is no doubt watching," she warned, looking up at the window where he had so recently stood. "She is already worked up over something, and I would hate to give her reason to have you thrown bodily from the house."

"That kind old woman?" Anthony quipped. If Ginny's news proved to be anywhere near as bad as his, this could be his last chance at levity. "Why, she's naught but an old softy! Had her reduced to tears, I did!"

"Grandaunt, weeping?" Ginny exclaimed with unaccountable pleasure. "Whatever did you say to her?"

"Merely that I could not wait to take you home to Dunsmere and make you my bride," he replied, carrying her hand to his lips. He waited, breathless, for the blush that would surely follow and nearly crowed in delight when she obliged him.

"Anthony," Ginny scolded, "surely you didn't! And even if

you had, she would more likely have rapped you over the head than weep."

He laughed. "You are right, of course, as always. Actually, I thought perhaps you would know far better than I what has reduced her to tears," he prompted, folding her hand into his own and giving it a squeeze.

"I'm afraid it was your mother," Ginny said with a sigh. "She was just here, and there was a bit of a row."

"Between m'mother and Grandmama?" Anthony asked, surprised. "How I wish I had been present to witness that!"

"No, you most assuredly do not! It was quite horrid. Lady Crenshaw called me a guttersnipe, and Grandaunt took great exception to that."

Anthony was astounded. "Surely you jest!"

"Why would I jest about such a thing?" Ginny snapped. Pulling her hand from his grasp, she stood and turned her back to him. "Your mother believes our engagement is at an end, and Grandaunt is persuaded it was she who made it so."

Anthony shot to his feet. "Grandmama did *what*?" The words that came next to his tongue were more eloquent, but as he didn't wish to blister the ears of his beloved, he bit his lip.

"I'm afraid she might be correct," Ginny said through what sounded like tears. "Grandaunt felt truly insulted and was quite adamant that, as a result of Lady Crenshaw's rudeness, I should not wish to take the name of Crenshaw."

"I don't understand!" He wanted to take her and turn her into his arms, but the rigidity of her stance said, "Touch me not." "That is, you didn't agree to that, did you? You do still wish to marry me?"

Turning to face him, she cried, "Of course! You know I do! It's only that everyone and everything seems against us, and I have to wonder if perhaps there is a reason. Perhaps they are all right. What if Lady Derby should do her worst? Perhaps people will cut me dead in the street and refuse all our invitations. What if our sons won't be allowed to attend Oxford or

Miss Delacourt Has Her Day

Harrow, and our daughters remain unwed, all because you married the vicar's daughter, no better than a guttersnipe!" Then she burst into gusty tears.

Anthony thought perhaps even Grandmama could not object when he pulled Ginny against his shoulder and wrapped her up in his arms. If Grandmama dared to try, she could very well go to the devil. What's more, she ought to go for making Ginny cry. His mother could go along, sooner rather than later. It would be a pity if she missed the wedding, but if it meant Ginny would be more comfortable, so be it. While he was at it, his uncle, the duke, should be added to the list of those consigned to hellfire. As things were, he hadn't the heart to tell Ginny what the duke had said in the course of their most recent conversation earlier that morning. Better for Anthony to share it all with her at a later date, though never was sounding better with each sob.

"Anthony?" Ginny asked when she was all cried out. "I do not think it is true that a duchess never weeps."

He laughed in spite of the knot of woe that bound up his chest. "Of course they do, my darling, and you shall make a splendid one someday," he soothed, drawing the green ribbon from the pocket of his coat and tying it into her hair. "There, now, you see? You are the very picture of a proper duchess!"

Ginny laughed. No doubt she was thinking her still-bare feet and shapeless dress were sadly at odds with his words, yet he most heartily meant every one.

Chapter Seven

"Mother, I would have a word with you!" Anthony bellowed through Lady Crenshaw's chamber door. He preferred that she had come down to the parlor when he first requested her presence, but her abigail had inferred that Lady Crenshaw was not at home, upon which he had charged up the stairs to rap on her door. She failed to open it, but he felt sure he heard a whimper of dismay on the other side. "I know you are in there. If you do not open this door, I shall set fire to it!"

The door swung open as if it had been lent wings. "Anthony, how dare you? I am your mother!"

"And I am the next Duke of Marcross, or have you forgotten?" he barked, hating to invoke his title but allowing anger to win out over integrity.

"Of course not!" she said, all the while avoiding his gaze. "It's only that I am persuaded you were once possessed of some manners. I do not know what that girl has done to you, Tony, but I do not like it."

"I do not see as how I should be a slave to manners when you, Mother, are not." It was Ginny who had helped him learn that manners were for mankind, not the other way around. "Now, do we stay in the hall, or shall we retire to somewhere more private?" Without waiting for her reply, he took her firmly by the elbow, steered her into the sitting area of her chamber, and closed the door with a loud *snick*.

Miss Delacourt Has Her Day

He was dismayed when she wrested free of him and disposed herself on a small sofa, arranging her skirts around her in the artifice he despised.

"Mother, tell me it wasn't you who taught Ginny to do that," he begged. "You will be the ruin of her. Perhaps I *should* cry off."

"But of *course* you should, Anthony! Have I not been saying so all week? As if I could ruin her. Why, there is nothing left to ruin!" she exclaimed, spreading her hands wide. "Your grandmother has seen to that. She could have been passable, even unexceptionable if handled right. As it is, she will ruin *you* if she has not done so already. You are too good for her."

"It is she who is too good for me, madam!" In fact, Ginny had saved him. It had taken only five minutes in her company for him to realize how utterly bored he had been, how futile his existence. The days he had spent quarantined with her at the Barringtons' had been the most fruitful of his life, and he had willingly given up all he had held dear in order to ensure she would continue to be his guide throughout his life. None of it would have happened without Grandmama.

"That's another thing. I understand you insulted my grandmother in her own home!"

Lady Crenshaw dabbed at her eyes with a scrap of fabric fringed with a quantity of lace. "As she insulted me!"

"Yes, but she did not have her broom, er, carriage called out for the express purpose."

"Anthony, you know I did not! I went to Wembley House to speak to your Miss Delacourt, a young woman clearly possessed of great intelligence. I felt if she knew how all of Society is up in arms about this mésalliance of yours, she would see the wisdom in bowing out of your life."

"Mother, do tell me you did not prey on her lack of experience with the *ton* in order to twist matters in her own mind? You know that my marriage to her, to anyone else, or, lacking a willing bride, failure to marry at all whatsoever, would be nothing but a seven-days' wonder. You have her thinking that I would be far better off marrying someone such as Lady Derby."

Tilting her head, Lady Crenshaw worried her lip with her teeth and gave him a narrow look. "Did she say so? Has she agreed to cry off?"

Anthony, appalled that he had come from such loins, slammed his hand against the nearest wall. "No, she has not! Should she ever feel the need to do so, I can see to whom I should credit the blame!"

"You find fault with me now, Anthony, but you will soon come around to my way of thinking. You will be thanking me in days hence—see if you will not!"

"Mother, would you truly rather see me wed to Rebecca? Does your standing in Society take such precedence over my happiness? True, I thought my heart broken when she made her preference for a title so cruelly clear, but my sorrow was but a day compared to a lifetime of grief I would be forced to endure should Ginny not be by my side." Anger spent, he sank into a chair and put his head into his hands. "It would be a grief beyond bearing, one from which I could not hope to recover." Straightening, he looked his mother in the eye. "Is it for that I should thank you?"

Lady Crenshaw sniffed. He would be sure to tell Ginny that as more proof that duchesses do cry but thought he ought to test the waters a bit. "Mother, are you softening toward my case, or are you sickening with a cold?"

To his surprise, she sprang to her feet and rushed to his side. "Oh, my poor darling! I hadn't realized—truly I hadn't! You know how much your happiness means to me. Why, I have always done everything in my power to make smooth the road of life for you. I merely saw the girl as an unnecessary bump ahead for you, but if you must have her, I will learn to love her."

Anthony raised an eyebrow. "Truly, Mother? I own, I'm a bit taken aback. Two minutes ago Ginny was quite beneath my touch, and now you are at *aux anges* to welcome her into the family with open arms! As much as I dislike myself for it, I feel a frisson of doubt."

"Truly, my boy!" she vowed, sealing her words with a kiss to each of his cheeks. "Now that this bit of unpleasantness is over, I am anxious to ask you what your uncle had to say about things. I confess I was so distraught with regard to the hobble Lady Derby witnessed at the Hadleys' that I had him informed of it before first light. I assume he insisted on your presence bright and early? Was he terribly beside himself over the whole affair?"

" 'Beside himself' hardly does it justice, madam." Anthony sighed. He would much rather be sharing news of his difficulties with Ginny, but after learning the whole of his mother's behavior this morning, he was more determined than ever to keep the truth from his intended. "Let's just say he was a good sight louder than a man in his sickly condition had a right to be."

"Well!" his mother said in a conspiratorial manner. "You know your uncle. He always must be shouting about something. It's no wonder his heart has very nearly given out, just like your papa's."

The giving-out of hearts was not a subject Anthony found comfortable at the moment. Standing, he began to pace the confines of the narrow room decorated in every version of yellow. Everywhere he looked were shades of canary, champagne, saffron, citron, and lemon. Even his mother's morning gown was a pale, buttery gold. It was no wonder his stomach was growling; the room was a veritable tea tray!

"Are you hungry, my dear? I shall ring for Cook. No doubt your uncle offered you nothing at all whatsoever, and after summoning you to his side so early! And as for that grandmother of yours . . ."

"I would thank you to leave her out of this!" he retorted. He would do better to leave at once before he crossed the line with his mother, but he was too hungry to care. Meanwhile, it wouldn't hurt to mend fences a bit while he waited for sustenance.

"It would seem my uncle will condone my marriage to Miss Delacourt only if I perform three tasks to his satisfaction."

"That sounds simple enough. What are you to do?"

He flicked a speck of dust from the sleeve of his dark blue coat while attempting to suppress his impatience at his mother's machinations. For all her words of encouragement, she no doubt hoped they would be tasks beyond his scope and powers, as indeed they were. "He would have me triumph at a bout of boxing."

"Oh, well, that shouldn't be difficult. You were always a dab hand at boxing."

"You flatter me, Mother, and, as you well know, I can hardly fight just anyone. It would look as if I were fighting over Ginny's honor, and that will never do. That leaves only my instructor, Gentleman John Jackson himself, the most renowned pugilist in England. What chance have I in besting him?"

Anthony thought he saw his mother bite back a smile but could not be sure.

"Next, I must race a carriage and four at nineteen miles per hour or more."

"Never say so! None but the old Duke of Queensbury has ever even attempted a race at such speed."

"Do try not to be so full of glee," Anthony drawled. "Of course, Old Q had the blunt to have a specialized carriage made, one that was equal to the task. He ran the nineteen-mile course in rather less than an hour, in point of fact. I could never hope to do as much."

"And the third task?" she asked.

"I am to land a hot-air balloon on a specified target without aid of instructor or expert."

His mother, who had deigned to sip some of her hot choco-

Miss Delacourt Has Her Day 67

late, began to splutter with laughter and attempted to cover it with a bout of coughing.

"I do believe you are sickening with something, after all."

"Oh, Tony, you must own, it is above all things droll! Don't assume I am laughing at your plight. I said I would learn to love your new wife, and so I shall. I can't say the same for your uncle, however. So, when do you begin to accomplish the impossible?"

"I don't. I will marry whom I wish, when I wish. There is nothing my uncle can do to me, please him or not."

Lady Crenshaw was aghast. "But, Anthony, won't you even try? Your uncle can hardly disown you—you are the rightful heir, and the estate and title are all entailed—but he can most certainly make life a terror for you. I know he has done so for me!"

It was true. As long as the duke lived, as his heir, Anthony was beholden to him. If the duke summoned him to his side a hundred times a day, Anthony would be hard pressed to deny him. The fact that he was newly wed would doubtless only prompt his uncle to make even larger forays into Anthony's time, time better spent with Ginny. Perhaps his mother was right. It might not hurt to try if it bought him favor in his uncle's eyes.

The decision made, Anthony and his mother, in perfect harmony with each other, made merry over the baked eggs and ham cakes. On a full stomach, the problem of his uncle and the threat of Lady Derby and all she might do seemed a faint menace. Anthony turned his thoughts to preparing for his round of boxing with Jackson and to when he might again see his beloved.

"Is Almack's not open for dancing tonight?" he asked.

"But of course! That would be splendid! Has your Miss Delacourt procured a voucher as of yet?"

"We have only been in town but a few days, *ma mère*. I am

persuaded that Grandmama could acquire one, but since you are bosom bows with Lady Sefton, and she one of the patronesses of those hallowed halls, I thought perhaps it would be expeditious if you paid a call on her this afternoon."

Lady Crenshaw paled a bit, a circumstance that surprised Anthony not one whit, as it was at Lady Sefton's rout that Lady Derby had opened her budget with regard to Ginny and her unseemly behavior. "Well, yes, I shall see what I can do. You must own, Anthony, it shall be a bit of a struggle. I wouldn't be surprised if they revoked *your* voucher after your uncouth ways at the Hadleys'."

"Hmm," Anthony murmured. "I am thinking perhaps an elopement might be in order." He lifted a well-manicured hand and regarded his nails. "Who needs Lady Sefton when you can have a Scottish blacksmith sanctify your vows in a trice?"

"Oh, very well!" Lady Crenshaw said with an exasperated air. "I shall have her voucher here for you this evening, but you must promise to bring Miss Delacourt to dinner with you before the dancing."

Anthony inclined his head in agreement. "And you must keep my uncle's tasks for me a secret. My Miss Delacourt has had her peace cut up enough for one day."

"You can be quite sure I shan't breathe a word."

Anthony left his mother's abode in Berkeley Square more in charity with her than he had been in some time. His heart lightened by her promise to procure Ginny a voucher to Almack's, he turned his steps toward his preferred florist to order a posy made up for his beloved. She would no doubt wear white, as would the other young girls making their come-out this season, so he decided blush-pink roses to be just the ticket to bring out the color of her dusky cheeks.

He imagined how pleased she would be with his plans for the evening: dinner *en famille,* dancing at Almack's, and perhaps a stolen kiss or two in the shadows of the darkened parlor at Wembley House before bidding her good night. But first, he would visit Gentleman Jackson's Boxing Academy on Bond Street. He had some training to do.

By the time the posy arrived at Wembley House, Ginny was already dressed for the evening in what promised to be her favorite gown of the season. It was once again white but much more to her taste than the satin she had worn to the Hadleys' the night prior. The underskirt, a medium-weight silk in the palest blush, was topped with magnolia-white, petal-soft silk, fine and delicate as a spider's web. The bodice was the same magnolia over blush silk with tiny puffed sleeves and a low décolletage. A narrow blush satin ribbon was tied around the high waistline. It put Ginny in mind of the Maiden's Blush roses in Grandaunt's garden, white with a hint of palest rose in the center.

"But why are you not wearing your lace fichu?" Grandaunt demanded as she bustled through the door, a posy in her hand. "You must remember what I said about showing too much décolletage in an establishment such as Almack's. We wouldn't want the patronesses thinking you too fast."

Ginny thought this speech wholly characteristic of Grandaunt in light of the fact that the low neckline had been upon her insistence in the first place. However, the arrival of Anthony's note early in the afternoon stating his intention to escort them to Almack's that very night had sent Grandaunt into such a pother, off they had gone to the Pantheon Bazaar to purchase a lace fichu for Ginny's gown.

Grandaunt thrust the posy into Ginny's hands and drew the fichu from its place on the dressing table. "Where is that girl of yours?" she demanded while tucking one end of the lace into the neckline of Ginny's gown, wrapping it around her neck, and tucking the other end in like the first. "She should be doing this, not I."

"Yes, of course, Grandaunt, but Nan has just gone to fetch the curling tongs from the kitchen. Are these from Anthony?"

Ginny asked, indicating the little bouquet of roses she held clutched in her hands.

"Yes, they are, and they couldn't be better matched to your gown. Now," Grandaunt said as she took the posy from Ginny and deftly began to disassemble it, "this is how it is done. You wear a few buds in your hair just so," she said, lifting her squab-like frame onto her toes and holding the roses against Ginny's brow. "Your girl can affix those once she has curled your hair. Next, you pin one or two along the sash at your waist like so."

To Ginny's utter amazement, Grandaunt herself fetched a pin from the table and made short work of the task.

"Lastly, you take what is left, tie it up in a ribbon, tuck it into your décolletage, and voilà!" Grandaunt exclaimed, stepping back to survey her work.

Ginny regarded herself in the pier mirror. "Grandaunt! How lovely! But do you not think the fichu and the roses together are a bit much?"

"Pshaw! I am well aware what the young girls think of wearing a lace fichu in tandem with a ball gown. I felt very much the same when I was your age. However, trust me, it will be most commendable in the eyes of the patronesses at Almack's. Besides which," she added with a wag of her finger, "the roses will put everyone in mind of the fact that, though many shall have the honor of dancing with you, your foremost admirer is none other than Lord Crenshaw. We mustn't allow anyone to forget that."

Most especially not Lady Crenshaw or that odious Lady Derby, Ginny thought. What Ginny herself was to think of the puzzling status of her engagement, however, was something else.

"Grandaunt, I do not wish to give you cause to feel I have anything in my heart but gratitude for all you have done for me. However, if your words this morning have made worse my case with Anthony's family, I think it best for me to know my standing before I sit down to dine with his mother."

Miss Delacourt Has Her Day 71

There was apprehension in Grandaunt's eyes in spite of her vain attempt to hide it. "Is this public declaration of his affection not enough?" she asked, indicating the roses. "You are to dine with his mother. She has procured for you vouchers at Almack's!"

"Yes, Grandaunt, but I know so very little of Society, even still. People are forever doing what is kind and polite, and I just as often allow myself to be drawn into their net, only to find I am quite unwelcome, after all."

"Harrumph! Do not forget, Lady Crenshaw is the widow of a mere baronet. My dead duke outranks him any day of the week," Grandaunt declared. "Why, do you not think I could procure a voucher for you with but a snap of my fingers? As my relation, you are unexceptionable in every way." With this, she bent a fierce look on her great-niece. "As long as you do not forget yourself and say something completely beyond the pale."

She heaved a sigh and stepped back for one last look at Ginny's immaculate ensemble. Doubtless, she was pleased, for she smiled and said, "You must know, my dear, all has been forgiven: the unfortunate beginning of the season—I'll be the first to admit you did not take well—and your hasty retreat to the country earlier this month. No doubt, even the contretemps at Lady Hadley's last night has already been forgotten. What power Anthony's mother has to stir up trouble is but a puff of smoke in the face of your charm and eminent suitability."

Ginny bit back a smile. She knew her grandaunt was doing her valiant best to assuage her own fears as well as Ginny's, and she loved her for it. "Thank you, Grandaunt! Ah! That will be Nan at the door. I must hurry and finish with my hair. It is very nearly time."

"You are most correct, my dear," Grandaunt said. She opened the door to allow Nan's wide-eyed passage into the room and was gone before Nan could bob a curtsy and murmur, "Your Grace."

Ginny could see that Nan was full to bursting, but all she managed to say was, "Well, I never!"

"She does seem a bit subdued, does she not?" Ginny said with a wry smile. "She is still smarting over Lady Crenshaw's use of the word *guttersnipe*. I wonder what sobriquet she will have for me tonight."

"If my eyes have anything to say about it, I daresay she will call you beautiful," Nan replied. "But first, we must curl your hair."

Ginny sat obediently in the chair and watched as Nan turned her long, thick hair into a casually disordered arrangement of curls, braid, and bun. Once the last roses were fastened into the curls, Ginny surveyed her appearance in the mirror. She was pleased with every detail except one: the fichu. Against the soft cream of her gown, the crisp white lace was almost loud and competed for attention with the posy of roses nestled in her décolletage. She pulled the fichu from around her neck just as a rap came at the door announcing Lord Crenshaw's arrival and left it, forgotten, on the dressing table.

Chapter Eight

Anthony stood at the bottom of the stairs and waited for Ginny to descend. It mattered not how many times he laid eyes on her, each time was more breathtaking than the last. Her beauty grew alongside his love for her, and nothing, not even his grandmother's reproaches, could budge him from his spot.

"Anthony, you look a fool, standing there like some mooncalf! Come into the parlor as a proper gentleman should and have a drink. I certainly feel the need for a restorative in light of who shall be my hostess this evening."

"Strangely, I no longer find any benefit in alcohol, Grandmama," Anthony replied without taking his eyes from the upstairs landing.

"No benefit in alcohol? If I didn't know better, I should think you expect to live on nothing but love!" Grandmama retorted, but she was to have no reply to her impertinence, for Ginny had appeared at the top of the stairs, and the roar of the blood rushing in Anthony's ears drowned out all other sound.

As he watched her gracefully descend, a sudden memory of how she had looked that day in Grandmama's study less than four weeks prior rose into his mind. She had been so becoming in her green gown, it was the first time he had actually noticed she was beautiful. Yet, the Ginny of the green gown was but a caterpillar compared to the butterfly that flitted its way down the stairs in all its soft, white glory.

The knowledge that this beautiful, virtuous, intelligent, generous-hearted girl loved him in return made him feel as if he could slay dragons. So the duke wanted him to best the most famous pugilist in England in a round of boxing. What of it? So what if the duke demanded that Anthony win an impossible race? With love as his wings, he'd do it. A flight in a balloon? Done! Nothing was impossible compared to one impossible truth: Ginny Delacourt loved him not for his title or his wealth or his perfectly tailored and exquisitely made clothes but for who he was. For himself alone.

So startling was this thought, the breath caught in his throat. The pain of Lady Derby's rejection he had taken such care to keep alive and caged in his chest, the same pain that Ginny had beckoned forth during those early days of their courtship, had flown farther and farther away with each throb of his love-swollen heart until this moment, this time, this place. As she reached the bottom step and put her hand in his, he felt the cage door swing shut, enclosing love where once there had been only hurt.

"Anthony, what is it?" Ginny asked. "You look as if you've never before seen me."

"No, I don't believe that I have," he said, tucking her hand into his arm and escorting her toward the drawing room. "That is to say, I've never seen you looking as utterly enchanting as you do this evening."

"Do you mean that?" she asked, her eyes aglow. "I do so love this gown. Not quite as much as my wedding dress, but . . . oh, dear!" She clapped a hand to her mouth. "I have spoken out of turn. Grandaunt insists, as a matter of course, that you mean to marry me but I . . . I . . ." She turned and pulled him aside before they entered the drawing room in full view of Grandmama's watchful eye. "I can't be entirely sure what is safe to assume and what is not," she said in a low undertone. "Not after all that has been said and all that has not. Grandaunt seeks to assuage my fears by claiming you would not have sent the roses if you did not wish for everyone to learn of your attachment to me."

"She is exactly right," he said, bringing her hand to his lips in order to keep his gaze from falling to the little bouquet tucked into her dress. "My uncle has tasked me with one or two chores"—*three, to be exact*—"before I formally announce our betrothal, but they will be the work of a moment," he said with a snap of his fingers.

"Anthony!" Ginny cried, her eyes pools of horror. "What has happened to your hand?"

Too late he remembered his bruises from the bare-knuckle boxing he had engaged in with Gentleman Jackson earlier in the day. If only he hadn't handed off his gloves to the butler. "It is nothing—just some sporting among myself and some, er, friends," he said as breezily as he dared. It was not uncommon for a gentleman to avail himself of a round of boxing. The Prince Regent indulged in the sport on a regular basis. Anthony hadn't the slightest reason to feel guilty. Nevertheless, keeping the truth from Ginny as to his motive made him uncomfortable. He wondered if perhaps he had better tell her of the match scheduled between himself and Mr. Jackson for the next afternoon, then thought better of it. There would be time and plenty after they were wed to divulge the truth to her regarding his uncle's unreasonable demands.

"It is indeed fortunate that we are off to dine *en famille*. At least *their* appetite won't go begging once they see your bruised hands, as surely they know of your proclivity for boxing, though I must own, I did not." She took his arm to lead him into the parlor, just as the sparkle in her eye and her arch smile took him to task for the oversight.

"There are many things about my grandson you do not know as of yet, Ginerva," Grandmama intoned. "He has trained in boxing since he was a very young man and, I have been told, even excels at it."

"Thank you, Grandmama," Anthony said with hopes she would

perceive that his gratitude for her explanation extended beyond her simple compliment.

"I am pleased to know you are among the best," Ginny replied, her eyes shining. "But I should hate for you to damage your face again so soon, ah, that is to say . . ." Ginny blushed and looked away in a fit of charming confusion.

He knew she was thinking of the first time he had kissed her during those early days of their quarantine at Rose Arbor. She had kissed him in return, then thrown a book at him, landing him a hefty lump to his forehead. Though enticing in the extreme, it had not been the proudest moment for either of them. He assumed Ginny had no greater wish than he for Grandmama to learn about that particular set of circumstances.

"If it please you," he said quickly to cover Ginny's discomfort, "I shall give it up entirely." That was to say, after the bout tomorrow. He would have to be sure to avoid any punches thrown at his face, but if he were even half as skilled as Grandmama claimed, he should manage rather nicely. "I believe it is getting late. We ought to be on our way to Berkeley Square."

Wraps, gloves, and Anthony's hat were brought and donned, and after a short carriage ride, Lady Crenshaw's house on Berkeley Square hove into view.

"This is passing strange," Anthony mused. "Dinner is meant to be a small affair, but the avenue is thick with carriages."

"That saucy Countess de Lieven resides down the street," Grandmama said with a huff. "Doubtless she is having her own dinner party before doing her duty as patroness of Almack's tonight."

Anthony wished to believe her explanation, but the sight of Lady Derby alighting from a carriage directly across from his mother's front door gave him pause. "Do beg pardon, Grandmama, but it would seem you are incorrect." Reaching for Ginny's hand, he gave it a squeeze. "It looks as if there will be a few more guests to dinner tonight, but never fear, the dancing shall be all ours."

Miss Delacourt Has Her Day 77

Dinner, alas, was not. When Anthony, Ginny on one arm and Grandmama on the other, entered the parlor, it was fair to bursting with guests. Lady Derby, who was entertaining the attentions of a pair of young bucks, came first to eye, while his mother was soon spotted in the act of attempting to foil the nefarious intentions of a gray-haired lothario.

Across the room, the sofa was taken up by a grim-faced man of the cloth doggedly conversing with a wan young woman, one whose resemblance to the former Lucinda Barrington was remarkable. Too remarkable. Gad, it *was* Lucinda! Quickly, he scanned the room and determined that her husband was one of the bucks enjoying Lady Derby's sphere of smiling approval. No wonder Lucinda was out of sorts. What game was his mother playing, and how might he thwart it before it was too late?

"Ah," he said, testing his voice for telltale tremors, "I think it best if we leave." Grandmama, her mouth opening and closing like that of a blowfish, was at a loss for words. It was a first in Anthony's memory.

"I think not," Ginny said with surprising calm. She looked directly into his eyes, and he saw no fear in them. He dared to flick a glance at Lady Derby, who simpered at him over her cordial of canary. No fear there, either. His mother, on the other hand, was making herself as small as possible in the shelter of the gray-haired man's imposing girth. It couldn't be Everston, could it?

Shaking free his arms, he was across the room in two strides. "Mother, I would have a word with you."

"Anthony!" Lady Crenshaw cried with a shaky little laugh. "Have your manners gone begging? You do not give Lord Everston his due."

Anthony inclined his head. "Everston, I do beg pardon, but I must have a private word with Lady Crenshaw."

Everston bowed and moved away.

"Mother! *Him?*" Anthony cried. "Of all people, how could

you? You know how Grandmama detests him. Look how he corners her even now."

"Anthony, I will not be dictated to in my own home! It is my dinner party, and I shall invite whom I wish."

"Ordinarily, I would agree with you wholeheartedly. However, dinner was meant to be just the four of us. You know how I have been counting on you to make Miss Delacourt feel a welcome part of the family."

"Yes, she is most naturally welcome. Only a dinner party of three females and one male would be uneven, don't you agree?" she asked with a snap of her fan, behind which she hid her face from the company at large. "I invited Everston for your grandmama. They are both getting on so in age, don't you think? Mr. Graham neatly rounded out my numbers. However, when Lady Derby got wind of it, I could hardly claim it was family only and felt I must invite her, as well. And then . . ."

"Mother!" he hissed. "The undesirable presence of Lord Everston pales in comparison to that of Lady Derby. How can you not perceive that? What of the feelings of Miss Delacourt?" he urged, but Lady Crenshaw had already moved away and did not benefit from his words.

Drawing a deep breath, he took stock of the situation. Ginny had placed herself between the crotchety cleric and Lucinda, who doubtless felt a measure of relief by the act, as she was now wringing out her much-abused handkerchief rather than employing it to stem a tide of tears. Grandmama had wrested herself from the clutches of Everston, who watched her greedily over his snifter of French brandy as she greeted Avery and drew his attention to his woeful wife. Anthony's mother had disappeared, which left only Lady Derby and the last male guest. With a start, he realized it was Simmons, a much-disliked schoolmate from Eton. As Simmons was the son of a mere baron, Anthony assumed Lady Derby's flirtations were only useful in marking time.

Realizing what his mother intended for the evening, he felt

his hands curl at his sides. Seating at the dinner table was ordered by precedence, dictating that he and Lady Derby should walk into dinner together and be placed side by side. Ginny would be left to sit below the salt with the dour preacher, a man he had never before seen in his life. He wondered where his mother had dug him up. Scotland was as good a guess as any, but he rather doubted even his mother's reach went quite so far.

He knew Ginny's wits and charm would get her through any unpleasantness with the prim and prosy preacher, but he was more doubtful about her reaction to his own dinner partner. Memories of the rather strained meals he had endured during the quarantine at Rose Arbor threatened to do away with his appetite altogether, especially when he considered the presence of Lucinda. For some unaccountable reason, dinner at the Barringtons' almost always involved dropped napkins, clattered forks, or shattered crystal. Perhaps such imbroglios went unnoticed in the provinces, but here in town they were likely to be a matter for much discussion.

Shuddering, he began a mental inventory: napkins, not much to fear there; spoons he could deal with; forks, knives, and crystal goblets, all heavy and inclined to be sharp. Dinner plates! He hadn't any experience with how far or accurately a laden dinner plate could fly, and though he enjoyed the broadening of his horizons as much as any man, he rather doubted flung china would improve anyone's character and certainly not his mood.

At risk of being maudlin, Anthony added Avery to the list of possible sources of unpleasantness. One mustn't forget his penchant for tears à la carte or à la anywhere, for that matter. The fact that their last conversation had involved being called out by Avery—a tiresome habit of his—was a fact that returned to Anthony's conscious memory in full force. Though he would much rather point a pistol at Avery than endure his tears, he preferred weeping to risking Lucinda's imagined indisposition becoming the topic of conversation at dinner.

There was nothing for it. It was time to leave. He went immediately to Ginny and took her by the hand.

"The bell has not yet rung," the preacher protested with a strong burr. "I have been enjoying the company of this fair, wee lass," he said with a clap of his hand to Ginny's arm, "and I won't part with her until I am made to."

Anthony's gaze flicked from the preacher's black-rimmed fingernails, which stood out in strong relief against Ginny's fair skin, to her face. To his surprise, she gazed steadily back at him with wry curiosity in her eyes. It would seem that Ginny had had enough of tears, as well. Despite her willingness to brave every affront, even the attentions of the loathsome minister, Anthony wanted nothing more than to leave and to do so with as little fuss as possible. Silently, he drew the glove from his hand, shockingly bruised as it was, and once again took Ginny's hand in his.

He heard the gasp of alarm she dutifully swallowed before she addressed the man seated at her side. "I am persuaded, Mr. Graham, you won't begrudge me a moment with Lord Crenshaw." She honeyed her words with a smile.

The smile was lost on Mr. Graham, however, whose whole attention was given over to the red and purple bruises covering the knuckles of Anthony's hand.

"Mr. Graham," Anthony said with a fractional bow of his head. "It would seem there's another just like this one. I would be most pleased for you to make its acquaintance if you are so inclined," he added in a low purr.

Mr. Graham withdrew his hold on Ginny's arm and clasped his hands tightly together in his lap. "Fists are not the weapon of a gentleman," he said gruffly. "I prefer the use of pistols myself."

"For that, I fear, you shall have to get in line," Anthony drawled; then, drawing Ginny to her feet, he led her swiftly to a side table and poured himself a drink.

"Did I not overhear you tell Grandaunt only this evening

that you no longer have a taste for alcohol?" Ginny asked with an arched eyebrow.

"Did I?" Anthony said in a voice that sounded curt even to his own ears. "It looks as if I spoke too soon. At any rate, we must depart," he said, pulling her paisley shawl up around her shoulders. "I'll fetch Grandmama, but you must head straight for the stairs."

"What? Because of that poor minister?"

"Yes." He shook his head. "No! That is to say, I made a mistake in bringing you here tonight." He had trusted his mother to make Ginny a part of the family. However, in light of present company, it was clear she had never intended to do any such thing. If the promised voucher for Ginny to Almack's appeared, he would eat his hat. Worse, the longer they stayed, the greater the chance that his dear mama would let slip the details with regard to his trio of odious tasks, the ones he meant to keep from Ginny at all costs.

He saw her face crumple a bit and congratulated himself on his decision to quit the house. Her tears were more endurable than Avery's, but he had no wish to start them flowing anytime in the near future.

"No tears tonight. I'm afraid I left my handkerchief at home, and Lucinda's already looks the worse for wear."

Ginny opened her mouth to respond, to say he knew not what, for she was spared the effort of formulating a reply when the dinner bell rang. Mr. Graham shot instantly to his feet, whereupon, to Anthony's dismay, Ginny took the preacher by the arm and went with him into dinner.

Chapter Nine

Ginny regretted her decision the moment she took her assigned seat between Mr. Graham and Mr. Simmons, who was of an age with Anthony but seemed much younger with his flighty ways and shallow observations. Sadly, her conversation would be limited to him and the dour minister, since speaking across table was highly improper at a formal dinner, even if one were betrothed, albeit somewhat secretly, to the man seated directly opposite. Meanwhile, she would be forced to endure watching as Anthony limited his conversation to the ladies at either side. Lucinda and Lady Derby were two of a pair; both bore the title of countess, a head of lush blond locks, and an expression of coy defiance.

The fact that Anthony had once been attached in one way or another to each of them, however falsely, did nothing to quicken Ginny's appetite or her confidence in her own upcoming nuptials. Neither did the initial hurt that had assailed her when Anthony was so eager to hasten her away from this paltry clutch of "high Society." Even so, that had faded enough to make way for curiosity. Though she was tempted to believe he feared she would say or do something unsuitable, she knew him well enough by now to suspect that something else was afoot. She took a sip of the soup course, a light broth seasoned with garden herbs, and waited.

"Miss Delacourt," Mr. Simmons said with an ingratiating smile, "I understand you are newly come to town."

"Yes, indeed," Ginny replied. It seemed better to leave unsaid the fact that she had been in town and presented at court at the beginning of the season, before that fateful fortnight spent quarantined in the country. "I find I am enjoying the parties and balls a good deal more than I expected." She stole a glance across the table to see appreciation for her remark in Anthony's eyes but was surprised to find only wariness.

"Oh, do you not enjoy dancing, Miss Delacourt?" Mr. Simmons parried with a significant glance of his own at Lady Derby.

"Who does not?" she asked but owned to herself that it very much depended on with whom one was dancing. She could not prevent her eyes from once again straying across the table but this time was genuinely startled by Anthony's grim expression. If she didn't know better, she would hazard a guess he would like nothing better than to fasten Mr. Simmons' hand to the table with a fork.

Lady Derby's expression, however, was one of unaccountable mirth. Ginny bit her lip in consternation and spooned more soup into her mouth.

"Well said, my dear Miss Delacourt! You acquit yourself well on the dance floor, do you not?" Mr. Simmons asked.

Ginny pressed her napkin to her lips, giving herself time to think. Mr. Simmons, whose gaze had slid from her face to her fichu-deprived décolletage, seemed to be baiting her, Lady Derby was clearly in on the joke, and Anthony's face was quickly becoming the immobile Society mask she had been at such pains to animate not many weeks hence. Quickly she called to mind everything she knew about dancing, table talk, and polite conversation in general, but none of what she had said so far seemed the least amiss.

She took a deep breath and looked a question at Anthony.

There was thunder in his eyes, and he gripped his spoon with a heretofore-unknown savage intensity that, sadly, did nothing toward offering her a clue as to what he would have her say.

"Come, Miss Delacourt, surely you dance better than you converse?" Mr. Simmons asked with a harsh laugh.

Willing herself not to blush, Ginny hastened to reply. "I acquit myself well enough, but no doubt my skill, or, perhaps, lack thereof, has created a bit of a stir now and again." She thought her answer the best of both worlds—not too pretentious or self-abasing, as either could invite scorn. She was disabused of this notion when Lady Derby went into gales of laughter, drawing the attention of the whole table, even Lucinda's, who had heretofore been wholly engrossed in flirting shamelessly with her own husband.

Noting the expressions of dismay on nearly every face, Ginny suddenly remembered what she had forcibly pushed from her mind—the altercation on the dance floor at Lady Hadley's only the night before. None of it had been any fault of hers, and though Anthony blamed her naught, she couldn't help but feel she was being made an object of fun in his place.

Ginny imagined this was but a taste of what life with a country wife would fully contain. No one would dare insult Anthony outright, but she feared the jibes, the veiled contempt, the mild but insolent remarks would follow him wherever he went. Could a man who had so recently chosen love over the approval of Society bear the brunt of such treatment?

She met his eyes across the table and read the answer there; he would bear it only as far as she and not one whit further. She smiled in relief at his generosity and was rewarded with a smile of such tenderness, she thought she might weep. It gave her the strength to endure whatever Lady Derby and her ilk had in store, and she had begun to think on an appropriate reply, when, with a loud scraping of chair legs against the marble floor, Anthony rose to his feet.

Miss Delacourt Has Her Day 85

"Grandmama, Miss Delacourt, I believe we are expected elsewhere."

"Anthony, what is this?" the dowager duchess demanded.

"I believe we have outstayed our welcome, Grandmama. It is time we were off to our next obligation."

There came more scraping of chairs as Lady Crenshaw sprang to her feet, followed by the remaining men at table. "Anthony, what can you be thinking? Do sit down and enjoy the rest of your dinner!"

"I am afraid I cannot. The food is excellent, as always, but I cannot say the same for some of the company," he said with a challenging glare for Mr. Simmons, whose gaze was still hovering in the vicinity of Ginny's décolletage and so did not benefit from it.

Ginny noted that Lady Derby had the grace to look affronted, but it was Lucinda who jumped to her feet. "How dare you?" she cried. "How could you say such a thing to me after all we have meant to each other?"

"I second that allegation!" Lord Avery cried. "Er, that is to say, if someone were to challenge you to a duel, I would happily act as second!"

At those words, Anthony let go of all semblance of composure. "This is all that was wanted," he mumbled into the palm he scraped across his face. "Lady Avery, if, by your words, you allude to a sham engagement that lasted for all of two days, I must remind you that what we had did not amount to two sticks to rub together."

There was a loud gasp from a number of people at table.

"Anthony, you never told me you were betrothed to Lady Avery!" Lady Crenshaw cried.

At the same moment, Lord Avery was issuing his own instructions. "Come, my flower," he said as he took Lucinda by the elbow. "We know when we are not wanted."

"No, Eustace! I wish to stay," Lucinda said with a stamp of

her foot that betrayed her penchant for making herself the center of attention.

"But, my darling," Lord Avery crooned, "how can we countenance such a slight? It is above all things fortuitous that I am already due to duel the man. All that is wanted is to round up a second, and the deed is done."

"A duel?" Lady Crenshaw cried in unison with Ginny, who sprang to her feet to join the majority of dinner guests already standing. Sadly, the footman hovering at her back with the intention of serving up the next course did not anticipate such a flurry of activity and was forced to jump back with a yowl. Anthony collapsed into his chair with a groan just as the dish the footman had been holding crashed to the ground, leaving the calf-foot's jelly to quiver en masse on the floor.

Heart pounding, Ginny dared to meet the gaze of all assembled. Lucinda feigned ignorance, turning her exquisitely pointed chin in the air, while Lord Avery's chin quivered along with the jelly. Doubtless, it was his favorite dish. Mr. Graham looked studiously in the other direction and utterly missed the fact that Lord Everston was seen to lick his lips. Lady Crenshaw, her eyes agog and mouth agape, clutched a napkin to her chest while emitting a silent scream. Mr. Simmons and Lady Derby, the few guests who remained seated, were at pains to hide their mirth. As for Anthony, well, she dared not look at him.

Just as she summoned the courage to determine her grandaunt's reaction, the old dame pushed back her chair with a long, lingering scrape of wood on marble, the footman who stood behind her being too stunned to do his duty in aiding her.

"Deborah, I thank you for your hospitality," she said with a perfectly regal air. "However, I believe my grandson was quite correct in that we are expected elsewhere."

"Your grandson?" Lady Crenshaw shrieked. "I will remind you that he is *my* son! I won't have him abandoning me in the midst of my social function!" She turned to pin a demanding glare on her son, who appeared to be at great ease, his hands relaxed on the arms of the chair and his impassive gaze fastened to the bucolic painting of sheep grazing in a field hanging on the wall just beyond Ginny's head.

Ginny thought he took a good deal of time in formulating his reply but owned she could not blame him. She wished, ardently, that she could snap her fingers and disappear, but the chaos left in her wake would doubtless remain, a thought she could not tolerate. Looking once again to her betrothed for guidance and gaining none, she did the only thing she could; she took up her napkin and bent to the floor to begin work on the closest mess at hand.

"No!" Anthony shouted, jumping to his feet with a violence that sent footmen all over the room recoiling in alarm. "A duchess does not scrub floors, Miss Delacourt!"

Ginny, stung to the quick, rose on her heels and came face-to-face with Anthony as he bent over the table and braced himself with his bruised hands splayed against the white tablecloth, his head nearly level with the wine goblets. His face, however near, was as inscrutable as ever.

"Ginny," he said, as if she were the only other person in the room, "it was in my mind to say that the only opinion that mattered to me was yours."

"And mine!" Lucinda interjected with a pout.

He continued speaking without giving Lucinda so much as a glance, but his jaw tightened, and a vein at his temple began to throb. "That by your word we would stay put or quit this house. However, I find I cannot honor your request if you should wish to remain. I must insist that you come away with me this moment."

Ginny, deciding it more suitable to tend her wounded heart at a later time, made her decision. She wasted no time in dropping the napkin in favor of the hand he lent to her aid and rose gracefully to her feet. "Lady Crenshaw," she said with a little bow, "I am most grateful for your abundant hospitality."

Without adding his words of gratitude to Ginny's, Anthony stalked over to retrieve his grandmother, then returned to Ginny's side to draw her hand through his free arm.

Lady Crenshaw gasped. "Anthony, truly, you do not mean to leave? Why, I have not yet served the main course!"

"Then I suggest you do so before it grows cold," Anthony replied in a voice no more than tepid.

Lady Crenshaw turned her indignant gaze on Ginny. "If you think I should deign to so much as broach your name to any of the patronesses of Almack's," she said in a voice of awful finality, "you are more a fool than I surmised!"

It was in awful silence that they turned to quit the room, though Ginny was startled to see the wry smile that puckered Anthony's lips at his mother's revealing pronouncement. She was, however, utterly confounded by the way he tucked his head between his shoulders—until she heard the sound of shattering glass. The knowledge that Lady Crenshaw was the sort who threw objects was sobering, indeed, and she vowed to never again throw anything for as long as she should live.

The click of the dining room door closing behind them had barely registered in Ginny's ears when a strident voice was heard to rise above the babble of voices around the table. The voice could belong to none other than Lucinda, who was inclined to make herself the victim in every tragedy, and it was growing closer.

Anthony tightened his grip on Ginny's arm and quickened his step just as Lucinda flung open the door. "How could you desert *me*, Lady Avery, a countess, to such ruthless company?" she cried.

Ginny heard a groan but couldn't be sure if it came from Grandaunt or her grandson, who quickened his pace even further. There came the pitter-patter of dancing slippers striking the floor as Lucinda gained ground, and soon her dainty gasps of breath could be felt on Ginny's shoulder. Lucinda scurried along just behind them in full harmony of flight as they fled down the stairs and out the front door, Lord Avery's cries of "Where are you going, my flower?" trailing after them all the way out to the street.

Once they had gained the walkway, however, their flight petered out to a full stop. As there had not been time to request that their carriage be brought around, they were forced to wait until it appeared, Grandaunt huffing and puffing, Lucinda making indignant remarks such as "How *could* they!" and "Do they not know I am a countess?" as if she were the injured party in this contretemps, while Anthony paced and looked everywhere but at Ginny. This delay allowed Lord Avery all the time needed to appear at their elbows just as they were about to clamber into the carriage, his arms full of wraps, gloves, hats, and a cunningly worked silver flask Ginny had never before seen but which, unaccountably, was claimed by Grandaunt Regina.

To no one's surprise, Lucinda swept her way into the carriage the moment the opportunity was provided, though both age and title dictated that Grandaunt should go first. With a *tsk* of annoyance, Anthony helped his grandmother inside and stepped up after her to steady her until seated, then put his hand out the door to assist Ginny, whom he drew in to sit by his side. This left Lord Avery with the choice of expecting the short in stature but generous in girth dowager duchess to make room for him or to take his place next to Ginny.

Ginny wasn't sure if she should feel grateful or a bit put out when he chose to sit next to her. As it was, she was mostly breathless as she was forced to endure the carriage ride, thigh to thigh, as it were, with two handsome gentlemen of fashion. Try as she might, her mind *would* stray to inappropriate topics of observation, such as the difference between Lord Avery's limbs, which she imagined to be as soft and white as his hands, the pudgy kneecaps nearly lost in the surrounding flesh, and Anthony's long legs with their corded thighs, sculpted calves, and firm knees. What's more, his temptingly broad shoulder was the exact height against which to rest her cheek.

"Where are we off to?" Lucinda asked. One could always leave to Lucinda the task of cutting through the thickest of silences.

"Almack's," Grandaunt tersely replied.

Lucinda made a small moue. "I shall enjoy it vastly, I'm sure, but I doubt Ginny can find anything in it to like."

Lord Avery gave a sharp bark of laughter. "What, you find you cannot abide stale cake and orgeat any more than the rest of us, Miss Delacourt?"

"I suppose I shall find out," Ginny surmised.

Lucinda furrowed her pretty brow. "I can't see how you could possibly have a chance to taste either."

Anthony placed his hand over Ginny's, the one clutching the edge of the leather seat between them, as a means to limit the unintentional brushing of her leg against his. "By that if you mean to suggest that Ginny shall be so occupied with dancing that—"

Ginny was never to learn his objection to the idea of her dancing so often and long that no food or drink would have the chance to pass her lips, for Grandaunt, who had returned to her usual poised and regal self, cut in with her own pronouncement.

"Lady Avery makes a point. It seems that, despite our hostess' promise, she failed to secure a voucher for Ginny, making entrance to the building and thereby the cake, orgeat, and the dancing," she added with a nod for her grandson, "ultimately denied."

Ginny felt awash with shame. "I realize I don't always do and say what I ought, but I have been trying, so *very* hard, to be pleasing to everyone." She turned to Anthony and beseeched him with her eyes, but he did not avail her of his expression. She felt it to be another small blow to her heart in an evening full of them. Blinking back tears, she asked, "Have I, even then, been found so lacking?"

"It is not the patronesses who have found you lacking," he said, his voice choked with anger, "but my own mother who has failed to petition them on your behalf. I suspected her treachery when I learned with whom she had invited us to dine tonight."

Finally he turned to Ginny, but it was too dark to read the expression in his eyes. Taking her hand, he put it to his chest and, covering it with his own large and bruised version, held it tightly against his heart. "I swear to you that I knew naught of this. I would have done anything in my power to spare you every indignity you endured this evening. And in the home of my mother! It is a betrayal beyond contemplating. I, who have been toiling in the service of all that is right and proper in the eyes of Society for far too long, to have been the unwitting instrument of this so public humbling of your character is a circumstance beyond my enduring."

His stock of words finally depleted, he plucked her hand from his heart and kissed it with such tender fervency, she felt she must forgive him every hurt she had ever sustained, tonight and beyond. This was *he*, the man behind the mask, the Anthony she had yearned to know and had almost begun to fear she had lost.

He put her hand once again to his chest. "Can you forgive me, my most beloved Miss Delacourt?" he asked in a voice free from all restraint.

Nodding, she whispered, "But of course," and felt her heart fill with joy until she thought it must burst into shafts of pure light. When he drew her close, she willingly nestled within the circle of his arm, against his soft, black suit-coat and stiff, snow-white cravat, with shocking disregard for her fellow passengers. Indeed, she forgot they were even present until the sound of Grandaunt Regina's voice broke through the façade of isolation that held them so in thrall.

"That will be quite enough, young man! Have you forgotten? Ginny is under my protection. I will not have her treated like Haymarket ware mere moments before her debut at Almack's. What will Sally Jersey have to say to that?"

Her debut at Almack's? Ginny felt her heat skip a beat. Was it possible Grandaunt had performed some kind of miracle? She found she wanted to go to Almack's above all things. Stale cake and orgeat were nothing to anticipate with any great amount of pleasure, but one did not willingly concede an evening of dancing with her beloved.

"What is this?" Anthony asked, his voice rumbling in his chest beneath her ear.

"*This*," Grandaunt said with a triumphant flourish above her head, "has been in my possession all day, courtesy of Countess Esterhazy."

"Yes, but what is it?" Lucinda asked with a moue.

Hardly daring to believe it was true, Ginny sat up and snatched a ticket from the dowager duchess' hand. "Oh, Grandaunt, thank you!" she cried.

"You are more than welcome, my dear," Grandaunt replied with a pleased air.

"Yes, but what *is* it?" Lucinda demanded.

"This," Ginny announced, "is my voucher to Almack's!"

Chapter Ten

As they entered the hallowed portals of Almack's, Anthony wondered what had possessed him to bring Ginny to such a place. True, it was the surest way to imbue a young woman with a certain éclat, as merely being allowed to enter would give Ginny's reputation some much needed polish. However, it was also full of gentlemen on the hunt for a wife. It might have been his imagination, but he was persuaded that every male in the room turned toward the door the moment Ginny made her appearance. The room was also filled to brimming with women intent on making their daughters the wife of a future duke. The thought filled him with a pale anxiety compared to the clutch of fear that gripped him when he realized how Ginny would be perceived by the male population: fair game.

"Grandmama," he whispered, "do you think this the best idea? Ginny might feel a bit out of her depth here."

"Don't be absurd, Anthony! We have arrived but a moment ago, and she is vastly enjoying herself already.

Anthony had to agree. Ginny's expression was lively as she took in every detail of the large room, with its glittering chandeliers, enormous gold-framed mirrors, and sumptuous velvet window dressings, much of which were barely discernable through the masses of the richly adorned assemblage. In light of Society's so recent rejection of her, prompting her flight into the country a mere three weeks ago, Anthony thought her willingness to brave more opportunity for censure somewhat remarkable.

"Well, then," Ginny said, "someone steer me in the direction of the dry cake. I find I am a bit peckish after that entire spoonful of soup I swallowed at dinner." She looked to Anthony with glowing eyes. "Shall we?"

Anthony opened his mouth to agree, when Lord Avery, who was hovering nearby, stepped forward and offered Ginny his arm.

"Allow me, Miss Delacourt," he said with an ingratiating smile for Ginny. "My lady wife is desirous of a bit of a cose with you, and I find I cannot deny her anything."

"If you insist, Avery," Anthony said with a disobliging air. "But, mind you, I shall be 'round directly to collect her for the next set." He knew his reticence to see her walk away between Avery and Lucinda was ridiculous. He could hardly sit in Ginny's pocket all night even if their betrothal had been posted in the papers. Though he wished to dance with no one but his beloved, he knew she would be considered "fast" if she devoted all of her dances to him. If she were courageous enough to come to so public a haunt after all that Society had done and said to make her feel inferior, he had better do his best to ensure that her appearance at Almack's worked to her advantage.

Turning to his grandmama, he said, "I believe I see Lady Jersey just on the other side of that potted palm. Does Ginny not need her approval before she is allowed to dance the waltz?"

"I do believe you are right, Anthony. It has been so long since I sponsored a young girl's come-out, I am not yet wise to all the ways of Almack's."

"Be that as it may, dearest," he said with a slight bow, "you are wise in the ways that matter. I don't believe I have yet thanked you for your foresight in obtaining Ginny a voucher."

"Tut-tut," Grandmama said, scanning the crowd. "Of course

I obtained the voucher. She is my responsibility. At least until such time as she becomes yours," she scolded.

Rather than feeling put off, Anthony felt an utterly unfamiliar and complete harmony with his grandparent that filled him with such a warm wash of affection, he nearly leaned in to buss her raddled cheek. Instead, he put his fingers to his beaming lips and gave her a nearly imperceptible wink from the corner of his eye. She blushed like a veritable schoolgirl, and he obligingly looked away, glad for an excuse to rake his gaze over the crowds in hopes of spotting Ginny. However, he was not done visiting the subject of the voucher.

"At risk of sounding ungrateful, Grandmama, I would like to ask why you failed to mention your possession of it when so many opportunities to do so were laid at your feet." He turned to smile into her eyes, a trick he had long ago learned would soften her pride. "May I?"

"You may ask, but I am persuaded you will not like the answer," she warned.

Sighing, he busied himself with an imperceptible mote of dust that had the audacity to light on his sleeve. "Ah, Grandmama, you must think me quite daft. Blast me if tonight was not the truest proof of my mother's capacity for treachery. Surely there is nothing you can say that would oblige me to think less of her than I do at this very moment."

"It was not fear of your *mother's* frailties that stayed my hand," Grandmama said pertly.

Anthony froze. "If by that you refer to any uncertainty that Ginny will acquit herself with anything but grace and charm tonight, you are sadly mistaken," he said coldly, all his former amity having evaporated in an instant.

"Ginerva is the beloved granddaughter of my most loved brother," Grandmama replied in a huff. "I am willing to overlook her naïveté, her preference for outspokenness, as well as her talent for attracting trouble wherever she goes. I must admit, however, to some concern with regard to her ability to carry herself off to advantage." She turned and grasped Anthony by the arm. "But more than that, I fear what further rejection or an outright cut direct from the wrong person will do to her already lackluster reputation. I was never so glad that I had this voucher in my possession before the contretemps at the Hadleys', or I might never have had the means to bring your future wife up to snuff. I might have once been married to a duke, but my influence in Society grows weaker at the same rate my cheeks wrinkle," she said with a snort.

"I humbly beg pardon, madam," Anthony said, immediately repentant. "I should have credited you with more sense, as I know your desires for Ginny mirror my own."

"Most of them, anyway," she said with a wry smile. "Now, come, I see that Sally Jersey has finally left off conversing with that Mrs. Drummond-Burrell, whom I find I cannot abide."

Anthony proffered his arm for the trek across the room, all the while contemplating on the great quantity of personages Grandmama could not abide. More likely than not it was the other way around. However, it would appear that Lady Jersey was not numbered among those who cherished an aversion to the dowager duchess, as she instantly professed delight at granting the lovely Miss Delacourt the privilege of waltzing at Almack's.

"For, as you of all people must know," Lady Jersey gushed, "your Miss Delacourt is rumored to become the next Duchess of Marcross!"

Anthony felt the smile freeze on his face. "It would seem someone is telling tales out of school, Lady Jersey. Will you say who?" he asked, though he had a suspicion he knew the answer well enough.

"I don't see why not," she said with a lift of her chin. "I had it of the countess." Noting Anthony's obvious confusion, she hastily added, "Lieven, of course. I believe she heard it from your mother, my lord, or perhaps it was from Lady Derby. The three of them lunched together this afternoon—quite like the old days, wouldn't you say?" she added with a flourish of her fan. "Oh, look there, I do believe that is she with the Viscountess of Castlereagh now!"

Then she was gone, off to dampen the spirits of her next unsuspecting victim, Anthony silently mused. He and Grandmama exchanged a grim look, then hastened to find Ginny before she was accosted by Lady Derby and the obnoxious Mr. Simmons, who were even now making their way, arm in arm, directly for the supper room where Ginny was last known to be headed. The pair of them must have left their mutton to congeal on their plates in order to arrive so soon, and they, no doubt, were up to no good.

"For goodness' sake, Anthony, pick up the pace!" Grandmama admonished through puffs of rapidly dwindling breath. "Who knows what evil lurks beneath that crown of curls adorning Lady Derby's head? I knew that girl was trouble from the very moment I laid eyes on her, but your uncle *would* insist she was a good match for you," she muttered darkly. "Of course, Ginerva was practically in leading strings in those days, so how was I to know she was the one?" she asked, her voice rising in pitch. "Who was to know *any* of this would happen?"

"Who, indeed?" Anthony soothed. Who knew Grandmama could cover so much ground at such a spanking pace? Who knew the precise word to adequately describe the look in the eyes of those who feared they would be knocked to the floor with utter abandon? Who knew Grandmama would attempt to deprive Lady Derby of several locks of hair when she caught up to her?

It was fortunate, indeed, that Anthony deduced her intention and put a stop to it before more than a few onlookers perceived the dowager duchess' clawed fingers straining to grasp the hair at the nape of Lady Derby's neck.

"Grandmama," he hissed, taking her outstretched hand in his. "You grow hysterical!"

"But she will get to Ginerva before we do and cause some

hideous scandal—I just know it. We must stop her! Oh, how I would drag her to the ground if I thought I had the remotest chance of succeeding," she railed.

Due to the fact that, by this time, Lady Derby and Simmons had disappeared through the doorway opening onto the supper rooms, Anthony rather doubted there was anything either he or Grandmama could reasonably do but pray. Since he further doubted that, despite Almack's lack of alcohol, God took much notice of those assembled in party rooms, Anthony felt sure his prayers would go unheard.

Nevertheless, as he and Grandmama entered the room, he found himself praying in any case. It, however, did nothing to prepare him for the scene that met his eyes.

The room was chockablock with people, all of whom were staring down-table at Lady Derby, who appeared to be embracing someone. Good Lord, it was Ginny! Even more astonishing was the fact that Ginny was putting her arms about Lady Derby, as well. He noted, with a decided lack of surprise, how Lucinda was attempting to make herself part of the tableau by draping her diminutive arms around the neck of each lady and pressing her face into their shoulders. Off to one side stood a beaming Avery, smiling down on the three women as if they were the blessed Holy Family and he one of the three wise men.

Regrettably, there was nothing holy about whatever kind of mischief was afoot. It would seem that Lady Derby wished to be seen treating Ginny with kindness. However, true kindness was purely selfless, and Lady Derby was never that. Worried, Anthony led Grandmama to a quiet corner where he could assess the situation before making his presence known. A visual tour of the room told him what he wanted to know; Simmons was nowhere to be seen. He must be up to something, but what?

He hadn't the chance to think long on the problem, as Lady Derby was saying something to Ginny, something that was clearly causing Ginny great distress. Discretion might very well be the better part of valor, but Anthony hadn't the time to test the veracity of that statement. Instructing Grandmama to have something to eat, he moved at a pace slightly slower than a mad dash and reached Ginny's side in time to hear Lady Derby say something about a bet some gudgeon had made at White's Gentleman's Club. As "some gudgeon" was forever making bets at White's, this tidbit did little to hold Anthony's attention.

"Miss Delacourt," he said with nary an attempt at civility for Lady Derby, "I believe I hear the chords of a quadrille being struck. Would you honor me with a dance?"

Ginny shot him a look of pure gratitude before replying. "My lord, how kind! I was only thinking how much I love to dance a quadrille." Placing her hand on his arm, she allowed him to draw her away from a silent but haughty Lady Derby and out into the main hall, where the dancers were lining up to begin.

Once again, every male head turned to note Ginny's appearance. More disturbing, every female head did, as well. Such a deep hush fell over the room, it prompted the orchestra in the balcony to put down their instruments while craning their necks over the balustrade to observe what could be causing the lack of commotion.

Anthony was gratified to hear Ginny stifle a gasp before turning to him, a question in her eyes. She had demonstrated remarkable restraint during the course of a long and difficult evening, and he had never been more proud of her. Putting his free hand over hers where it lay on his arm, he gave it a squeeze. "It would seem Mr. Simmons has been busy. At what, I couldn't hazard a guess, though I would have to say it was most effective."

Ginny drew a deep breath. "I suspect there is a means to discovering his mischief. Meanwhile, as long as we are here, we might as well dance." She bit back a smile but could not hide the telltale signs of that maddening blush as it stole along her cheeks. "I confess I have been looking forward to the dancing with great anticipation all evening."

With formidable restraint of his own, Anthony resisted the urge to pull her into his arms and kiss her right there. "Dancing it is, then," he murmured, a tiny smile playing about his lips. He heard the breath catch in her throat and knew she had read the wealth of meaning in his expression. Leading her out onto the dance floor, he gave himself a mental shake with the reminder that a mere trio of impossible tasks stood between him and his wedding day. Three tasks, three days. Or less, if he could but manage to arrange it.

Twenty minutes of the quadrille went by too soon in spite of the torture he felt each time the pattern of the dance brought her to him in the nearness of a waltz, only to have it jerk her away into the rectitude of a minuet. Though she had eyes only for him, he knew she encountered goggle-eyed stares and disapproving frowns from every direction. Meanwhile, the dancers whose duty it was to meet up with her in the course of the steps behaved as gentlemen should but with an added circumspection that had him puzzling over the cause. Indeed, they seemed almost reluctant to so much as take her hand. No one spoke to her a single word.

When the dance was over, he led Ginny to the relative safety of Grandmama where she stood, red-faced and puffing in anger, along the perimeter of the dance floor.

"That was certainly enlightening," Anthony murmured to no one in particular.

"Was it? Why, then, do I find I am befuddled beyond measure?" Grandmama demanded. "If you are so enlightened, pray, enlighten me!"

"It would seem that further illumination is required," he replied, watching with great interest the progress of one of Ginny's quadrille partners as he crossed the hall toward the gaming rooms. He had stood out, not only because of his sadly out-of-fashion clocked stockings and shoes adorned with large

Miss Delacourt Has Her Day

gem-studded buckles, but because he was the only gentleman who had so much as smiled at Ginny since the distasteful scene in the supper room. Choosing him as the most likely to spare Anthony a word on the subject of the sudden chill toward Ginny, he excused himself from the ladies and headed off in the same direction.

As he made his way through the throng, he couldn't help but notice how the very women who had accosted him with their daughters less than an hour prior were now giving him a wide berth. Meanwhile, their formerly dispassionate daughters were now covering their blushes with their fans and batting their eyelashes fast enough to create a draft. Most puzzling of all was the young lady who slumped against him as he passed, leaving him no alternative but to catch her in his arms. Before he knew what was happening, she had peeled the glove from his hand and scurried off with it as if it were some kind of prize.

It was with no small amount of relief that he obtained the entrance to the card room through which the man with the clocked stockings had disappeared. Indeed, Anthony was immediately hailed by the fellow, whom he now recognized to be an acquaintance of so tenuous a connection, he couldn't recall his name.

He was standing with his back to the fire, a drink of something suspiciously unlike lemonade in his hand. "Sir Anthony!" he called again, waving an overly zealous arm over his head and startling the card players seated at the nearby deal table. "How lovely to see you! It's been an age!"

Anthony accepted the drink of unknown origin thrust into his hand. "If you can call our dancing the quadrille just now an age," he riposted, giving the liquid in his glass a wary sniff. Clearly there was something other than fruit juice circulating the room, as Mr. Clocked Stockings was drunk as a lord.

"Oh, beg pardon, it's Crenshaw now, is it not? Devil it is!" he bellowed without waiting for Anthony to respond. "Just met up with Irvine! You remember Irvine, do you not?" Again, Anthony hadn't time to respond one way or the other before his companion forged ahead. "Said you were ready for leg shackles, but I told him you weren't the marrying kind. Not as if you were in line to be a duke or anything!" He laughed uproariously, as if the means by which Anthony became heir to a dukedom was the most amusing joke he had heard all year.

"My cousin will be sorely missed," Anthony interjected before the fellow had a moment to recover his breath. "However, in light of recent events," he added without elaborating on which, "I must confess, the subject of marriage has become a more welcome one." Indeed, quite ardently desired, but there was no need to fill the prosy fellow in on those details.

His companion winked at him and gave a low coo. "She's a beauty! Trouble is, a beautiful girl like that, she's not likely to wait until the old duke is dead."

Anthony's smile froze on his face. "I beg your pardon?" He placed the alcohol-laced drink on the deal table with a loud *clink* and took a measured pace forward. "I am persuaded you wish to rephrase that statement, sir," he demanded in a voice as smooth as silk.

Unlike the men gathered around the table, the man with the clocked stockings was too drunk to sense danger. "You're a handsome blade and all that, but you might have to fight for her," he said with a wink.

"Oh?" His anger replaced by piqued interest, Anthony plucked his quizzing glass from among the folds of his clothing and tapped it against his chin. "There's talk of a fight, is there?" Could his uncle have been so foolish as to let slip news of his bout with Gentleman Jackson on the morrow?

"Oh, I can't say. It was Irvine who filled me in. Here he is now."

Suddenly, a man Anthony was sure he had never met, presumably Irvine, appeared at the first man's elbow and whispered something into his ear. "Come along, now, Winters," he said aloud with a nervous laugh. "You've had quite enough!"

Winters, who had turned white, allowed himself to be led away but not before both men darted covert glances at Anthony's hand, the one ungloved by the fainting maiden. After a moment of stiff silence, the men at the table resumed their game, allowing Anthony the chance to shoot his own subtle gaze at his hand, one of a pair liberally covered with bruises. Realization began to dawn.

Chapter Eleven

Ginny had had quite enough. It was one thing to be gazed at with expressions of admiration. It was quite another to have people stare at you through narrowed eyelids, naked curiosity stamped on their faces.

"Come, Grandaunt Regina, I believe we should find Lord Crenshaw and go home."

"Now, Ginerva, that will never do," Grandaunt huffed. "When you are a married woman, you will find that your demands will most likely fall on deaf ears. A man does not like to be dictated to."

Ginny felt as if she had been slapped. "Perhaps that was the way of it when you were a bride," Ginny retorted, "but Anthony is not cut from the same bolt of cloth as his grandfather."

Grandaunt sniffed. It was a far cry from the scolding Ginny expected in return for her disrespectful attitude. "I'll admit, things were different when I was young. Anthony is different, too, thanks be to that! I would never have thrown the two of you together, higgledy-piggledy, if I thought he might be disinclined to fall in with your wishes."

"Why, thank you, Grandaunt. You almost make me sound a perfect hoyden." Ginny, knowing she had let her tongue get away from her, dared not risk a glance at Grandaunt's face for fear she would look as hurt as Ginny felt. Taking a deep sigh, she softened her tone. "There is no need to assassinate my character. It's not as if he does what I wish at all times. If he did, the two of us would be dancing at this very moment," she explained, swallowing her disappointment as the strains of the waltz were struck. "Odious stares or not."

"You are quite right, Ginerva, just as you are quite right to trust him. There are things he might not make you privy to," Grandaunt said with a suspiciously offhand air even as she lifted her fan to shield her lips from passersby. "But there is nothing he would not do for you." She paused, then added, "There is naught that I have said these last three years during which I have clothed, sheltered, and guided you more worthy of your notice."

Ginny, struck by the giddy effect her grandaunt's words had on her state of mind, resisted the urge to ply her fan in front of her face in the coy manner exhibited by the more sophisticated girls in attendance. Yet there was something to be said for having the means to hide your blushes. Grandaunt's implication that Anthony was a man of secrets so weighty as to prevent him from unburdening them to Ginny was as enticing as it was troubling. The thought that he would do anything for her despite his other obligations, whatever they might be, was cause for blushes, indeed.

"Pray tell, what is it he is keeping from me?" she asked as soon as her wildly beating heart allowed her to speak. She found that dwelling on the "things he might not make her privy to" slowed the pounding most effectively. Indeed, the more she thought of his secrets, the more her heart froze in fear. Were they secrets as to Lady Derby? Did they have anything to do with their wedding or possible lack thereof? She was not to have a response to her question, however, for rapidly descending upon them was a visibly discommoded Lady Jersey.

"Oh, my dearest duchess, it's nothing to be concerned about, I'm sure, but I think it best if you were to depart forthwith."

"Depart?" Grandaunt demanded as if they hadn't only just been discussing the very same action.

"Yes, well, never fear. I am persuaded all shall be right as rain tomorrow. That is to say, next week. They do refer to these things as a seven-days' wonder, do they not?"

Grandaunt pulled herself to her full, though negligible, height, her back ramrod straight. "'These things'? To what 'things' do you refer, Lady Jersey?"

Unable to face the dowager duchess' glare, Lady Jersey turned her pleading gaze to Ginny. "Do, let's not make a fuss over this! It's not as if you have committed a crime, now, is it? I had everything fully in hand, deflected the wagging tongues at every, er, wag, but you must know that the place is abuzz with rumor and innuendo. If only you had worn a fichu rather than that trifling little clutch of flowers in your décolletage, all might be well. As it is, I find I cannot stem the tide as it is currently flowing."

Tide? Flowing? "What does my décoll . . . er, my flowers have to say to anything?" Ginny asked.

"Well, they are from *him*, are they not?"

"If by 'him' you mean Lord Crenshaw, yes," Ginny said, nodding. "However, I'm afraid I still do not perfectly understand you."

With a furtive glance about the room, Lady Jersey took Ginny and the dowager duchess each by the elbow and guided them to a less populated area. One closer to the exit, Ginny couldn't help but notice.

"You really don't know what is being bandied about?" Lady Jersey asked in amazement.

"Of course not!" Grandaunt cried, skewering Lady Jersey with a sharp look. "Who would dare to tell us?"

It seemed Lady Jersey would, for she immediately began to babble. "They are saying Lord Crenshaw has gone mad and attacked more than one man who dared to insult an 'unnamed lady.' They are saying he is secretly betrothed, as well. Surely they are referencing you, Miss Delacourt, but some insist it is Lady Derby for whom he has supposedly harbored a deep and abiding love. I am persuaded this is all a mistake due to his previous attachment to her, but one thing has led to another, and it is being said that Lord Crenshaw has taken exception to you due to your unsuitability. I have been going about championing your cause for what seems like hours, but I could not gainsay the objections of my fellow patronesses. If only you had tucked a scrap of lace into your bosom, I might have withstood their admonitions. As things stand, you are quite sunk below their esteem."

"I will have you know, Lady Jersey," Grandaunt said in a carrying voice, no doubt intended to be heard by the hateful Mrs. Drummond-Burrell, who stood nearby, "my niece had planned on wearing a particular fichu she had purchased for this very occasion, but I would have none of it. I insisted she instead wear the token of affection sent to her by an admirer, as his feelings are more at a premium with me than those harbored by the likes of some."

Lady Jersey's eyes grew wide. "My dearest duchess, if this admirer would merely put his stamp of approval on the relationship by contacting the papers with news of his betrothal, I am persuaded this shall all blow over in a matter of days." And then she was off, bustling after a passerby, crying, "Why, Carolyn, I *thought* that was you under that divine turban!"

Ginny sighed and waited until Lady Jersey had moved past hearing before thanking Grandaunt Regina. "For I do not know what I should have said if you had not spoken. I have never been more ashamed yet never less deserving of it."

"I do not fully agree, Ginerva. There is that matter of the fichu, after all. And to think I ordered out the carriage this afternoon for the sole purpose of acquiring it! However, seeing as my grandson has reappeared, I will hold my tongue for now. Meanwhile, I suggest you keep your chin up, my dear."

Curiously deflated by her grandaunt's admonitions, Ginny

pondered whether or not a single emotion had been left unexplored by her battered psyche during the course of the long evening. Though watching Anthony as he made his way to them filled her with a decided glow, it was the same warmth she experienced upon each occasion she saw him. True, he was looking more handsome than usual in his black evening clothes with that froth of linen at his throat. So handsome, in fact, she barely noticed when he stopped to converse with a cluster of women. She so loved the way he walked, elegantly, with his hands behind his back, she thought nothing of the fact that he stopped to exchange a word or two with every cluster of women along the way. She was so enraptured by the sweep of his brow over his richly lashed, radiantly blue eyes that she almost failed to think it strange when he stopped to reach into a bevy of women to pluck something from their midst.

Surprised by her realization that the something was a glove, she didn't turn away as he pulled it over his hand, then lifted his head to catch her gaze in his. So quickly did his mouth curve into a smile when he saw her that even once he had planted himself at her side, she quite forgot to ask why Mrs. Taggart-Elliot's daughter had possession of his glove in the first place.

"Anthony, it's about time you recalled yourself to your duties as escort," Grandaunt chided. "Ginerva and I find we are quite done in and wish to go home."

"Oh, but we mustn't. At least, not yet," Anthony demurred. "I have promised Miss Delacourt a waltz," he said with a slight bow in her direction, "and I am persuaded she will depart only if dragged by the heels unless she gets one."

Ginny was torn between glorying in her beloved's attentiveness and fretting over the fact that a waltz was coming to a close and another was not likely to be played for at least an hour. She felt sure she would break under the strain long before then.

"I can see you have him well trained," Grandaunt quipped.

"It is you whom I credit for his pretty manners and thoughtful ways," Ginny said with a fond smile for her grandaunt.

"And am I to receive no credit at all?" Anthony demanded with a playful air.

"I should say not. The waltz has been playing an age!" Grandaunt snorted. "It shall be over all too soon, in spite of your 'pretty manners.'"

"Then we had best hurry. Say you will dance with me, Ginny! Part of a waltz is better than no dance at all, is it not?" He looked so unblinkingly into her eyes, Ginny felt sure there couldn't possibly be a single secret lurking in his.

"I would love it above all things," she said, placing her hand on his arm. "They aren't any more likely to stare at us for joining the dance at the close than they have been already."

The second he swept her into the rhythm of the waltz, she knew she would not regret choosing to dance, even if only for a few moments. With her arm resting along the length of his own, they were as close to an actual embrace as one dared. The sensation of his arm muscles tightening and relaxing beneath hers as he guided her through the steps was intoxicating. Mere inches stood between the two of them, and she longed to lay her head against his heart and feel it beat, strong and sure, into her ear. It was the only thing that made her feel as if, at long last, she truly had a home.

All too soon, she heard the music come to a close, but when she began to move off the dance floor, he pulled her back into his arms, and they were once again circling about the room. Only then did she realize another waltz had been immediately struck and that the other dancers were just as astonished as she at the unexpected turn of events.

Throwing Anthony an incredulous look, she saw the truth in his expression of delight. "Lord Crenshaw, I do believe you had something to do with this," she accused him, her smile brilliant.

"Why, Miss Delacourt, how could you doubt me? My

'pretty manners and thoughtful ways,' however come by, aren't for naught!"

A bubble of joy welled up within her chest and escaped in a laugh. "As long as they are spent in currying my favor, I find I cannot object." Suddenly she found there was nothing that could touch her equanimity; not the secrets to which Grandaunt alluded, not the rumors to which Lady Jersey put tongue, not even the incriminating stares at the back of Anthony's head to which Lady Derby was even now so studiously applying herself.

All too soon, the dance was over, and it was time to depart.

"Do you wish to remain for a while?" Anthony asked, drawing her arm through his as they sauntered back to Grandaunt's proper purview. "If need be, I can get around Grandmama."

"What? And so misuse those pretty manners and thoughtful ways? I shall not hear of it. Besides, I would prefer leaving on a high note. One must admit that they were in short supply this evening."

Anthony seemed to take umbrage at that. "Never say so! Surely you haven't had your fill of insults and insolence. Why, just over there stands a woman whom I'm persuaded has not, as of yet, given you the cut direct."

It would seem their ensuing laughter was contagious, as Lucinda, who appeared suddenly at Ginny's elbow, was laughing, as well, and in an even more empty-headed manner than usual.

"I was just informing my wife," Lord Avery expounded from his place at Lucinda's other side, "that you wouldn't dream of departing without first collecting us."

"Indeed, we would not," Ginny assured him with a sinking heart. She had forgotten that the Averys had ridden hence in Anthony's carriage and would expect to be similarly conveyed home. She had been cherishing every moment of the blithe buoyancy between her and Anthony, but that bubble was burst the moment Lucinda appeared.

Grandaunt, by the time they joined her, looked entirely spent, the feather in her headdress askew and her face nearly as a gray as the silver beads at her neck.

"Oh, Grandaunt, you must be exhausted," Ginny soothed.

"And to think I had not one dance all evening," Grandaunt said, bristling. "In my day, my dance card was full continuously, and I never became so much as out of breath. Well, those days are done, that is plain to see."

"In that case, I shall take you home directly," Anthony insisted. "Avery, you won't mind should I take these two home before I convey you and Lady Avery to your residence?"

"It will be our pleasure to see the women home, won't it, my flower?" Lord Avery said, turning to Lucinda, whose only response was to emit a ladylike belch and giggle.

Ginny, attempting to quell the stab of disappointment that assailed her when she realized the carriage would consist of the five of them for the entire trip, refrained from speaking her thoughts aloud. Grandaunt's words of caution against dictating to her betrothed still burned in her mind. She was a bit mollified when Anthony allowed Lord Avery to lead with Lucinda on one arm and Grandaunt Regina on the other, leaving Anthony free to once more draw Ginny's arm through his as they fell into step behind the others and made their way out the door.

"I hope you don't mind, dearest. Grandmama looks done to death, and I think it best to get her home posthaste."

"I suppose that is for the best," Ginny said, managing a smile. "I find I am more tired than I thought, and tomorrow promises to be a most interesting day."

"Yes, I expect it does," Anthony said lightly, but a wary look sprang to his eyes, and his smile turned to a frown.

As they stepped outside, they were met by a sudden blast of chill air, prompting Anthony to put his free arm around his grandmother. Denied these last few moments of private conversation as the three of them huddled together against the damp, Ginny's former happy mood took a further turn for the worse. Every slight she had suffered during the course of the evening rose in her memory to goad her, yet most vexing of all was Anthony's frown when she mentioned her heavy schedule for the morrow. Had he forgotten she was to have another fitting for her wedding gown, after which there was more shopping to be done for her trousseau? Surely he didn't mean that she shouldn't occupy herself in such a manner. The entire subject was rather lowering, to be sure.

As these thoughts churned in Ginny's mind, Lucinda's babbling seemed never to cease, until each syllable she uttered felt like a nail being driven into Ginny's brain. By the time the carriage arrived, her foot had taken up a tapping that was a mere echo to the throbbing in her head. When Lucinda again dismissed Grandaunt's preeminence and was first to make her giddy way to her seat, Ginny was not inclined to look on her with the slightest degree of charity. Once they were all firmly ensconced, Lucinda's voice seemed to ring in Ginny's ears. It was "Lady Derby" this and "Lady Derby" that, until Ginny felt she might scream.

"Why, Lucinda," Ginny said through clenched teeth, "one would think you were drinking champagne all night, rather than mere orgeat!"

"Don't be a goose, Ginny!" Lucinda said with a slight slurring of words. "Everyone knows that *orgeat* is smuggler's code for *brandy*."

There was a stunned silence in the dark carriage, but Ginny felt sure she could feel a rumble of silent laughter coming from Anthony, who was seated by her side.

"Uh, my flower," Lord Avery ventured, "I was wont to tell you all evening; Lady Derby was merely twitting you."

"Twitting me? Why, how dare she? Eustace, I ask you, is it meet for a countess to be called a twit? And before you answer, might I remind you that her earl is dead while mine is still living?"

Miss Delacourt Has Her Day

"Yes, my darling, it would seem that it is so, but that is beside the point. She was not calling you a twit as much as she was, er, making a twit of you by telling you that monstrous lie."

"She lied to me, as well? Eustace, this is beyond enduring!" Lucinda wailed. Tears were not long in coming, and soon she was openly weeping. "Why am I expected to endure so much? Tell me, I beg you, about what did she lie?" she managed to ask between sobs of hysteria.

Ginny heard, rather than saw, Grandaunt throw her hands into the air in exasperation.

"Lucinda, you must get command of yourself," Ginny insisted. "Lady Derby was not lying, but she was being rather vexing. Orgeat is neither brandy nor Champagne. It is little more than the juice of an orange."

Lucinda's sobs stopped instantly. "Oh!" she said. "So, then I'm *not* inebriated!"

Even Lucinda was stunned into silence by that utterance, and the remainder of the journey was spent in peace. Ginny found herself wishing Lucinda would once again believe herself to be foxed and become verbose, as she longed to ask Anthony about his reaction to her wedding preparations, and the turning of the wheels was not sufficiently loud to disguise her words. However, Lucinda stayed uncharacteristically silent.

Ginny thought perhaps Anthony was finding the lack of communication as taxing as was she, for just as the horses rounded the last corner prior to home, he took her hand gently in his own and soundlessly brought it to his lips. Whether he forgot or refused to return her hand, Ginny did not know, but he kept it captive under cover of darkness until the carriage came to a halt.

Lucinda immediately moved to peer out the carriage window, even though it meant stretching herself across the entire length of the seat, the one currently occupied by Lord Avery and Grandaunt Regina.

"Oh, how lovely!" Lucinda cried without the typical clap of

her hands, so urgently were they needed to keep her from collapsing into her neighbor's lap. "I have never been to Wembley House when it is dark outside. Look at all of the lighted windows!"

Ginny found it difficult to frame a reply to such nonsense, as the tall, narrow, Georgian-style house was little different from the others on the square. However, it was the sudden appearance of Lucinda's slipper-shod feet in precariously close proximity to Ginny's nose that served most to rob her of speech.

"Lady Avery!" Grandaunt snapped. "Do recall your dignity, and allow me to alight. Why I was so inclined to share a seat with you, I will never know!"

"Oh, I do!" Lucinda cried as she regained her proper place on the seat. "It is because you deplore facing backward, as do I. As long as we are riding in the same carriage, we shall be seated together, as we both require the seat facing forward. Considering our great standing in Society, it is only proper, no?"

"Never again," Grandaunt riposted, her jowls quivering with indignation in the light streaming through the carriage window.

Apparently Anthony had anticipated trouble, as he had by this time alighted from the carriage and was holding out his hand for his grandmother, who, in turn, lost no time in wiping the dust of the carriage from her feet. Ginny, quickly following, found herself inside the house with barely a "good night" from Anthony before he turned on his heel and hastened away.

Going immediately to the window and pulling back the curtains, Ginny watched as he interceded for the groom in his attempts to convince Lucinda, who, it would seem, had insisted on alighting as well, to take her seat. Anthony succeeded where the groom had failed, and once the last of her azure-blue gown was gathered within, Anthony followed along after it into the inky black interior, whereupon the groom folded up the steps and shut the door.

It wasn't until Ginny was settled in bed for the night that she fell to turning over in her mind the puzzling events of the evening. Most perplexing of all were the odd things being said. First there was Grandaunt, with her implication that Anthony was keeping secrets. Then there was Lady Jersey's comment with regard to a wild rumor along the lines of Anthony's being crazed and attacking people. Anthony himself felt sure Simmons had been hard at work passing along some evil news. Could that have been it? Anthony did have bruises on his hands, but he explained them as being the result of a boxing lesson. Was this the unspoken truth to which Grandaunt Regina had alluded?

Blowing out her candle and pulling the bedclothes to her chin, Ginny decided it was all very troubling, and she was too tired to think on it before morning. It was as she was falling into a light doze that she remembered a crucial event. Lady Derby, in those few moments of amicable conversation earlier in the evening, had mentioned that a number of gentlemen from White's had taken out wagers with regard to a fight. Her manner was catty and her meaning clear, though Ginny had refused to believe it. Anthony would never agree to a fight over her honor and say nary a word to her about it.

Or would he?

Chapter Twelve

"Not again!" Anthony moaned aloud in spite of the fact that he was breakfasting alone in his Jermyn Street rooms. "What could the old man possibly want now?" The note had arrived on the same tray as his breakfast and the contents quickly scanned just as Anthony was plying his fork to tuck into a steaming dish of avidly anticipated plum cake.

Now the tea and cake would go untouched, for his uncle, the duke, had requested yet another interview. Not only would Anthony have no time to eat before dressing to meet the demanding standards of his uncle, he also found, to his dismay, that his appetite had all but fled. His boxing match was scheduled for that afternoon, but rather than using the morning to his advantage, there was nothing for it than to stand in front of a mirror while his valet turned his master out to perfection.

"Conti!" he roared loudly enough to be heard in the next room as well as those above and below.

Conti, the valet, presented himself in a trice, his arm bearing evidence of an uncanny prescience in the form of a stack of freshly ironed neck cloths.

"My lord? How might I be of service?"

"Surely you needn't me to tell you," Anthony said, glancing meaningfully at the snow-white cloths.

Conti hung the neck cloths over the edge of a chair and sniffed.

Miss Delacourt Has Her Day 117

"If you insist," Anthony said, flinging the note to the table and landing it, willy-nilly, in the plum cake. "It would seem I am to present myself to my esteemed uncle before my appointment at Mr. Jackson's. What he could possibly add to his previous admonishments, at this, the eleventh hour, I cannot say."

"Very well, my lord," Conti murmured, coaxing his master into a standing position and leading him to the nearby pier glass. "As usual, I shall strive to ensure Hees Grace has no need to puncture your pride with a diatribe on the state of your appearance."

"Any other day, Conti, and I would say the devil with the tie of my cravat," Anthony attested, despite the recoil of horror his words produced from the valet. "However, I mustn't allow the duke to undermine my confidence, not today of all days. Not only do I have a boxing match to win against my own instructor, but I have a carriage race to plan for tomorrow."

Conti made no reply, but Anthony took note of how the valet rolled his eyes behind him in the mirror.

"Out with it then, Conti. I know you well enough to suspect you have an opinion on the matter."

"*Sì*. I do!" he replied, pulling the first of what promised to be one of many ruined cravats from about his master's neck with a snap. "It ees thees. You are a fool!"

Gazing into the mirror, Anthony saw his eyebrows jerk up in surprise but refrained from scolding Conti before he heard what the man had to say on the subject. He attempted to gauge the valet's expression but was denied a view of his face, as he had turned to procure another cloth. No doubt this would be tied as well as the last but would be rejected in favor of some elusive notion of perfection present only in the mind's eye of the fussy Italian.

Impressed as much as he was baffled by the loquacious Conti's restraint, Anthony measured his words. "If indeed I were a fool, I doubt Miss Delacourt would have agreed to wed me. Unless, of course, you deem her a fool, as well?"

"No! She loves you. Love ees never foolish. As always, eet ees you who ees the fool. Was eet not I who informed you of the *buono* qualities of Mees Delacourt so many moons ago, *si*?"

"Yes," Anthony agreed on a sigh. Would Conti never leave off throwing that into his face? And would he ever be satisfied with his third or even fourth attempt at tying a decent cravat? "Nevertheless, I believe I am still at a loss. How is it that I am a fool?"

"Ah! That ees an easy question to answer," Conti said with a wave of his finger. "Thees fight, eet ees all wrong!"

Anthony bit his tongue and silently counted to ten before formulating a reply, a strategy he found himself employing often when conversing with Conti. "Let us go over the facts, shall we not? You have long averred that Miss Delacourt is the woman for me. Is that not so?"

Conti, busy tying his latest attempt, nodded.

"And is this fight not a demand of the duke? Am I not his heir? Am I not obligated to satisfy his deathbed request?" Anthony demanded, thrusting the valet's industrious hands away from his neck in exasperation. "In short, Conti, does this boxing match not elicit enough of a romantic notion to please even you?"

"But of course!" Conti insisted, catching hold of the dangling ends and resuming his work. "It is far more *romantico* than the *duello* last week with that *effeminato*!"

Anthony closed his eyes, shuddering at the thought of the scene that would no doubt ensue if Avery, the *effeminato* in question, were present to hear the valet's insult, however well aimed. Taking a cleansing breath, he started over. "So, I am a fool with regard to this boxing match. Why?"

"Because, my lord, you can never win! Eet ees above all things foolish to think you can best the premier pugilist in all of Eeengland! You might have had half a chance of beating him eef, perhaps, you had spent more time at hees establishment these last few years rather than riding and racing and, oh!" the valet said with a slap to his head. "The shooting! Eet is always the shooting!"

As this same argument had occurred to Anthony more than once and had kept him awake the better part of the night, he found he had no means of defense. It was just as pointless to claim that his time shooting had been time well spent in light of his having won the pistol duel with Avery only late last week; the guns had not been loaded.

"What, then, do you suggest?"

"Ah! Now you ask thee right question, my lord!"

"Conti, your ability to tie a cravat pales in comparison to your capacity to tie up a conversation in hopeless knots!"

"*Grazie*, my lord," Conti replied with a bow. "Now that your appearance ees satisfactory, I shall present to you my plan."

"I only pray the revealing of your plan takes less time than it did to ruin a dozen perfectly acceptable neck cloths. My uncle is waiting, and there is still my coat to don," Anthony pointed out.

"My lord," Conti said, hastening to produce the coat, "Hees Grace insists you fight a boxing match in order to win hees approval for your marriage to the *bella* Mees Delacourt. However, he did not say with whom you must fight."

Anthony was impressed but only with the wrinkle-free perfection of the coat as it slid over his arm. "In other words, I need only find someone who will agree to lose, and the deed is done. But who? I can hardly ask any of my friends to sustain an injury on my behalf."

"Agreed! Besides, eet must be someone who ees not a threat, my lord," Conti cautioned as he smoothed the fit of the coat over his master's shoulders.

Anthony gave his valet a dark look. "I am assuming by that you mean no one who merely *appears* to be a rival for Miss Delacourt's hand. Indeed, that would cause a great deal of talk." Fishing his quizzing glass from his jewel box, he hung it around his neck and proceeded to tap it against his lips in contemplation of the issue at hand. "Should I fight Gentleman Jackson, there would be no scandal. Why, it is done every day. Even the Prince Regent boxes against Jackson! However, should I fight anyone else, it will give credence to the rumors freely spilling about with regard to Miss Delacourt's honor. Therefore, I must fight a nobody."

"*Precisamente!* I am at your service, my lord," Conti said with a deep bow.

"You, Conti? I had no idea your regard for Miss Delacourt went so deep!"

"Eet does! Eet goes very deep, indeed, but my pockets do not," he said with a little sigh. "In fact, they are, at the moment, quite deplete."

Anthony was astounded. "Conti, even you could not have been so wise!"

"Yes, my lord, I am afraid eet ees so. The bets are made. I have arranged mine through the valet of the kind Sir Hillary, who has placed my wager in the book at White's in his own name."

Anthony pinned his seemingly omniscient valet with a gimlet eye. "Surely you are to lose this match. You have bet against yourself?"

"But of course, my lord! Eet would be a dishonor to Mees Delacourt should her betrothed fall to a mere valet."

"I see your concern for *my* honor can be measured only in the length of my shirtsleeves," Anthony said dryly.

"*Sì*, my lord," Conti said, his eyes rounded in question. "What else?"

Not for the first time, Anthony longed to elucidate on the obligations a valet owed his master, but the fear of a lecture from his uncle with regard to the virtues of promptness tempered his tongue. It would no doubt prove to be a fruitless conversation, in any case.

"Just be to Bond Street by two of the clock this afternoon, and I shall cry pax."

In no time Conti was through the door to his flat irons and boot blacking with a bow and a saucy smile. Anthony had dismissed valets for less, but Conti's penchant for anticipating a gentleman's every need was far too elusive a quality to disdain. This line of thinking left him with little to do but let himself out the door and be on his way to Hanover Square. However, just before the door latched behind him, he remembered something that gave him pause.

Hadn't that villainous Lady Derby said something to Ginny last night about bets? At White's? He had wondered more than once if Ginny had gotten wind of the boxing match but had finally decided she would have been unable to remain silent on the subject if she had. After all, Ginny was not one to keep her own counsel. True, she had said something about having a full schedule today. Could she know about the match? Could she even, in her adorable naïveté, be planning to attend?

Stepping back into his room, Anthony pulled out his ink pot and penned a note urging Ginny not to worry in the case that she knew about the fight and to under no circumstances go anywhere in the case she planned to make her way to Bond Street. Then he sanded, folded, and sealed it with a hearty congratulations for himself on doing it all in less time than it took to tie but one of the simplest of cravats.

"Conti! See that our Miss Delacourt gets this, *pronto!*" he called as he once again shut the door behind him.

The journey to Bond Street from Jermyn Street was a pleasant hour-long curricle ride, but Crenshaw House was that far again in the other direction. He would be three hours on the road, and all because his uncle refused to pay the frank for a letter. And why should he, when he could debase someone to his face? Anthony hoped the duke would be quick about it, as he had precious little more than three hours left before the scheduled match at Jackson's.

Lack of time was only one of many reasons Anthony was relieved when he was made to wait outside his uncle's bedchamber but a few moments rather than the usual half an hour. Another was the lack of life to this part of the house. Indeed, there was only shadow spilling its way along dark wood and cold marble. Perhaps, when he and Ginny were expected to make Crenshaw House their home, he would manage to convince the servants to allow him the use of his old room in a sunnier wing of the building. It was with this thought in mind that he was ushered into his uncle's presence and precisely why he was staggered to see the window draperies thrown back, allowing light to fall on every corner of the room.

"Crenshaw! How good of you to come!" the duke bellowed.

"Why, Uncle," Anthony asked in genuine surprise, peering into the shadows created by the voluminous bed hangings, "is that you?" Surely he hadn't so much color in his face the last time Anthony had seen him. And surely he had been lying nearly prostrate the last time he had seen him, as well, not lounging about as if he had been awake and alert for hours. Gad, the man was even dressed! In spite of his astonishment, Anthony couldn't help but notice the very fine cut of his uncle's shirt and the fact that his cravat was tied almost as well as his own.

It was with a little jolt that Anthony realized that, in spite of his uncle's poor health and wasted appearance, he was not as ancient as Anthony had always supposed. As the older brother of his own father, it would be safe to assume that the duke could very well be on the windy side of forty, and fifty could not be far off. Anthony had friends who were nearly as old and had not yet become fathers or even wed. It was an astounding thought.

Most puzzling of all was the leather valise on the night table in which the papers scattered along the counterpane had doubtless recently reposed. Curiously, it looked as if his uncle had been hard at work.

"Have I come at an inopportune time?"

"Oh, this?" the duke asked with a wave of his hand. "I'm just

Miss Delacourt Has Her Day

looking over my will. There might soon come a time when I will find it needful to change the contents, but that is neither here nor there."

"I see," Anthony mused, though he most assuredly did not.

"Don't fret, boy! I mean for you to get your due, regardless."

Anthony inclined his head. As the property was entailed and the succession ensured, his uncle's regard was extraordinary. "Is anything amiss?" He longed to add, "Anything other than your dying?" but felt the query a bit insensitive in the glare of his uncle's apparent hale heartiness.

"No, not at all. Why do you ask?"

Anthony opened his mouth to speak, but there were no words to be had. Resisting the urge to look about the room for an indication he had entered the wrong house entirely, he stood biting his lip and waiting while his uncle scribbled notes and cackled to himself at regular intervals.

Finally, when he could bear it no longer, Anthony managed to formulate an appropriate question. "Sir, have I come all this way for naught?"

"But of course! Now, do be off," the duke insisted. "I believe you are expected elsewhere. No doubt you'll be as late to your next appointment as you were to the last."

Too relieved to puzzle long over the strange interview, Anthony sketched a bow and turned to flee.

"I know what you're thinking, young man," the duke insisted, forcing Anthony to turn and face the long-expected tirade. "That I'm too old to know my own business. I know better what I'm about than a whippersnapper such as yourself. You leave my business to me, just as you had better be about yours!" the duke shouted, pounding his fist on the bed so that papers scattered hither and yon. "I meant what I said about that girl of yours, and I expect you to achieve all three tasks, or I'll find her a husband who can! Now scarper out of here, and have my man attend to me at once! At *once*, do you hear?"

Anthony heard, only too well. Gone was his suspicion that

someone had replaced his uncle with a younger, healthier version of himself. No one could read a lecture like his uncle, the duke, except perhaps Grandmama, and there was no mistaking one for another despite the startlingly similar sharply pinched nose they shared.

"Freestone!" Anthony bellowed in a dead-on imitation of the duke. Anthony prayed the hard-pressed valet would ascertain his master's need and wait on him forthwith. Meanwhile, Anthony was down the stairs and out the front door of Crenshaw House before one could say Jack Robinson.

It wasn't until he was safely behind the reins of his conveyance and had whipped up a smart pace for his return journey that he had leisure to reflect on how he was to carry out the three tasks upon which his uncle insisted before giving his blessing to Anthony's marriage. Surely his uncle's threat to find Ginny a more accomplished husband, one who could box and race and fly a balloon, was merely hot air. Grandmama would never allow Ginny to be packed off and wed to some old crony of the duke's. Or would she? Anthony shuddered. It was not worth thinking on. It was impossible. Indeed, it was horrifying!

Whipping up the horses to greater speed, he cudgeled his brain for a way to beat the greatest race time on record, one held by Old Q, the recently deceased Duke of Queensbury. The fact that the record, more than nineteen miles per hour for a chaise and four, was achieved sixty-five years prior was troublesome. The fact that no one had achieved that speed either before or since was irksome. The fact that the chaise in which this phenomenon was enacted was specially made with silk tracings and harnesses of lightest whalebone was worrisome in the extreme. By the time he arrived at Bond Street, he deemed it impossible to meet Old Q's time, let alone beat it.

However, he could not allow the possible fate of his second task to determine the end result of his first. Putting the carriage race firmly from his mind, he entered the boxing academy looking every inch the confident man his tailor would have him be. Jackson, of course, was a gentleman about the change in plans, and the kind Sir Hillary, along with all of White's, it would seem, was in attendance to see how his faux bet proceeded.

The fight was swift and satisfying. Conti went down in one blow, saving both his dusky complexion undue discoloration and Anthony's already much-abused knuckles the same. As Anthony pulled the valet to his feet amid cheers and jubilation from the spectators, his worry for the fate of tomorrow's feat returned in full force, denying him any sense of victory.

Conti, however, would not allow his master a moment to feel downcast. "Eef you have but the right question, my lord, I have the right answer."

"You have my utmost attention," Anthony adjured.

"Thees is not a question, but I will answer nonetheless. The daughter of the Duke of Queensbury!"

Anthony quelled an itch to hit the Italian enigma right in his aquiline nose. Again. "And how does this answer anything?"

"She, my lord, ees my cousin."

Anthony felt a lightness of heart so sudden, it threatened to create a great and abiding love for his obnoxious valet.

"In that case, what are we waiting for?"

Chapter Thirteen

Ginny sat at her dressing table puzzling over a note she had received shortly after consuming an excellent breakfast of hot chocolate and rolls. As unexpected as were the contents of the note, she had no doubt as to whom it was from; it was Anthony's seal impressed in the wax that held the missive closed.

"Why should he make such an odd request?" she murmured.

"Well, what does he *say*?" Nan insisted.

As it was her third query, Ginny refused to be nettled by her companion's cross demeanor. Ginny's reluctance to answer was due only to the fact that she found it difficult to speak when a deep apprehension had her throat so tightly in its grip. With trembling hands she lifted the note and once again read, aloud this time, "Go nowhere. I pray you, feel no anxiety on my behalf." She let the vellum flutter from her grasp. "Why should I not go where I have planned? And he doesn't say why I shouldn't be anxious on his behalf. It is a bit of a puzzle."

"Perhaps he spotted that man with the mangy ol' bear out and about today," Nan suggested with a shudder. "He knows how much it distresses you to see that chain about its neck. Why people hand over good coin to see such sights is one I cannot credit!"

"Nan, dear, I would gladly brave the bear in order to buy

my bride clothes, and I mean to dedicate myself to that end. Today! Besides which, I'm persuaded a mangy old animal is not so great a fear that he should feel the need to allay it. I think I might know what this is about, but I must go out to learn what I can."

"But, miss, he asked you not to!"

"Nevertheless, I shall go, and you shall accompany me."

"Me?" Nan asked, her eyes wide with horror. "I'm sure I wouldn't know what to say to anyone. It is the ol' dragon you should take along."

"Yes," Ginny said, turning to the glass to check her appearance one last time. "But I'm persuaded Grandaunt Regina would endeavor to keep me at home. Besides which, she knows what it is Lord Crenshaw refuses to say. What's more," she said, turning to bestow a warm smile on her friend, "you are in need of an outing!"

Nan cringed. "But the bear! I can't abide that bear, miss!"

Ginny bit back a smile, thinking it was high time Nan owned up to her fear of the bear. "I know you can't, dearest, which is why I shall fetch you a hat with a thick black veil from Grandaunt's room. You shan't be able to see a blessed thing."

"Well," Nan said, hesitating, "if I am to wear such a fine hat, I can hardly go out in my everyday clothes."

"You shall have one of my gowns," Ginny said, jumping from her seat and going to the clothespress. "Here; it's my black from when Father died and should fit you well, for all the flesh I've put on since. To think I used to be as rail-thin as you," she said with a *tsk*.

"Rail-thin, and no wonder Sir Anthony never spared you a glance," Nan exclaimed as she took the gown and held it against her scrawny form. "And here I am, still thin as a stick and you a regular go-er!"

"Now, Nan, there shall be no such cant if you are to ride with me today. Promise you shall be on your best behavior!"

"Yes, miss, o' course. I shall go directly and change."

Ginny collected her gloves, reticule, and paisley shawl, then donned her chip straw bonnet with the wide satin ribbon and tied it firmly beneath her chin. There was nothing like a lovely poke bonnet to protect one's complexion from the sun and one's carefully coaxed curls from being pulled this way and that by the wind, especially since she had requested the hood of the carriage be folded back. She would be more likely to spot any clues to Anthony's doings with the carriage fully open.

Once again she fingered the note and wondered exactly what it meant. In her heart of hearts, she knew he would never cry off, that he would move heaven and earth to marry her. Therefore, he could not possibly object to her shopping trip, at least not in and of itself. There must be some other reason he did not want her to go out, and the rumored boxing match was the most likely culprit. Whether or not it was the case, she fully intended to discover on her own.

John Coachman would doubtless have some light to shed on the matter, and the moment she was able, her hand in his as he handed her up the steps of the precariously swaying carriage, Ginny posed her question.

"Pray tell, where is the boxing academy in relation to Regent Street, where I am to do my shopping today?"

The driver scratched his head and surveyed her from the corner of his eye. "You don't want to be going there, miss. After two in the afternoon, Bond Street is only for gentleman. No lady of quality would be seen walking there."

Ginny settled her skirts around her and reminded herself she was to be a duchess one day. Holding her chin high, she said, "We needn't walk. I daresay a drive along the street past the boxing academy would do well enough."

The carriage dipped and swayed as the driver took his place at the box and turned to give her a rather imperious glance, one to which Ginny took great exception. For the first time she realized her expedition was a bit on the bold side, her dubious safety in

Miss Delacourt Has Her Day 129

the hands of this unknown quantity—minus Grandaunt's presence, no less.

"If ye don't mind me being so bold, miss, I would say a drive down Bond at this time of day would be the end of your 'opes and dreams to marry the young lord, though I'm meaning no disrespect, miss," the driver said with an obsequious tug at his forelock, an action at great odds with his assertive manner.

"Very well, then," Ginny said with what she hoped was an authoritative air. "In that case, might we merely come close? I hear there is to be a great fight today, and I am wishful of learning which of my friends will be in attendance."

There came a rumbling sound from the driver's seat that shook the entire carriage. As Ginny clutched at whatever was at hand to steady herself, she gradually realized the shaking was caused by the driver's laughter, and it seemed he was laughing at her.

"Miss, ye don't want to be seen anywhere near the place, and you ain't gots no 'friends' who are feebleminded enough to attend. It'll just be men. A proper young miss has no men friends, if'n you know wots I mean."

"Well!" Ginny said for Nan's ears only. "If it be that beyond the pale, Lady Avery is sure to be there with a feather in her cap." The thought of Lucinda having access to Anthony's activities while Ginny did not was a thought past bearing. Turning again to the driver, she attempted a different tack. "Is there a possibility of perhaps crossing over Bond Street on our way to Regent Street?"

"There's no other way but to cross Bond. There will be naught to see of the academy, though, unless we take Berkeley Street all the way down to Piccadilly so as to meet Bond at the right end. It'll take half-again as long, but it can be done."

"Oh, lovely!" Ginny cried and was relieved when the driver merely grunted and took up the reins to begin their journey.

"Isn't it exciting, Nan?" Ginny said, laying a hand on her companion's arm. "I promised I would take you along on many adventures if you would only come with me to London, and here we are! I shall buy you whatever you wish: ribbons at the Pantheon Bazaar, gloves if you like, even an ice at Gunter's on our way home. Oh, and we shall be sure to stop at Hatchard's Bookshop, as we shall pass right by it. I daresay I shan't have time to read a word between now and the wedding, but it will be nice to have a book or two at hand for later."

Nan groaned. "I think I shall be sick!"

"Oh, dear! We are going at a spanking pace, are we not? I daresay not being able to see is making things worse," Ginny said, lifting Nan's veil from her face. "We are sure to encounter no bears in this part of town, so you might as well be comfortable."

Nan sniffed. "I am persuaded it was yourself who was afeard of the bears," she said in her loftiest air. "I shall be just fine, now that I am able to look about."

"And I shall be just fine once I learn what it is Lord Crenshaw is at such great pains to hide from me," Ginny averred.

"Pain is what you'll get from that grandaunt of yours once you get home again. She'll not take kindly to your going off on your own this way," Nan warned.

Ginny hadn't considered the matter from that perspective but had to admit to the truthfulness of Nan's words. Grandaunt would be furious once she learned Ginny had gone off into the heart of London in the company of mere servants. The promise of any number of ribbons, even should they be every shade of old rose, had not the power to diminish the unpleasantness of Grandaunt's sharp tongue upon their return. Ginny pondered the matter and arrived at an excellent solution.

"I shall buy Grandaunt a gift, one that demonstrates how grateful I am for all she has done for me, and use that as an excuse to go shopping without her. I could hardly manage to surprise her by making my purchase right under her nose!"

Nan appeared to be unconvinced, but she uttered no more

objections, all her energy seemingly taken up in staying upright in the startlingly open carriage as the ground was eaten up at what seemed an impossible pace. This lack of conversation left Ginny free to muse on the events of the day. Though she was more than content to shop for pretty things and relieved to be having her final fitting for her wedding gown later in the afternoon, it was the boxing match in which Anthony was to fight that most occupied her thoughts. If she were not allowed to so much as saunter down Bond Street, how was she to learn anything of import?

Once they arrived at the corners of Bond and Piccadilly and Ginny took in the quantity of gigs, curricles, and carriages stopped in the street, her questions multiplied. What could everyone be doing here? Could the plethora of young bucks, corinthians, and dandies milling about be an indication of how far and wide rumors of the fight had spread? Ginny remembered that Lady Derby had mentioned the wager book at White's being filled with regard to who should be the victor of the match, but surely the members would prefer to await the results while ensconced in the comfort of their club?

"Have ye seen enough, miss?" the driver asked, his whip at the ready.

"I'm not sure. There's naught to be seen but carriages and a sea of black."

"I should say so!" Nan, who had replaced her veil, affirmed.

"I wasn't referring to your veil but to the gentlemen in their dark coats, Nan. There's not one lady to be seen in all that somber attire," Ginny said, craning her neck to spot a familiar face in the crowd.

"As long as the man with the bear is not among them, I don't mind the lack of color," Nan insisted.

"Miss?" the driver asked, holding his whip ever higher.

Just as Ginny was about to admit defeat, she heard a familiar voice coming from a carriage on the side of the road farthest from the seeming melee down Bond Street. Eagerly, she turned to put a face to the voice and was heartily downcast to be confronted with Lady Derby's contemptuous smile.

"What a happy coincidence!" she said. "Though, truth be told, I should have guessed we'd find you here. Young maidens from the country have very little sense," she purred. "And who is this you have with you?" she asked in a voice so cool, butter wouldn't melt in her mouth.

Ginny had never felt so bereft of speech in her life. Lady Derby was as menacing as ever, but it was the man with the hard, bright blue eyes seated beside her who studied Ginny's person with a cold insouciance that filled her with an icy sense of dread.

"Ah," she said, in a futile attempt to form actual words.

"Roxanne! Is that you?" Lady Derby exclaimed, addressing her words to the veiled Nan. "I had thought you said you weren't feeling quite the thing this morning."

The man said nothing, but his cold, bright eyes shifted and narrowed as he took in Nan's appearance.

Nan, blinded as she was, was thoroughly unaware she had been addressed and was silent, as well.

In a stroke of blessed good luck, Ginny remembered that the widow of Anthony's newly dead cousin was called Roxanne. Under the circumstances, it would not be entirely untoward for the two of them to be spending some time together. It was a scenario fervently preferable to being caught out in public with naught but a ruffian driver and an even younger maiden than herself with infinitely less town bronze. Sending a silent prayer of thanks winging upward, Ginny thought furiously. Lady Derby was the person who could answer her questions, and answer them she must!

"Yes, well, the two of us are out to fatten my trousseau but couldn't help but be intrigued by the crowd yonder. I wonder if perhaps a carriage tipped over, and all of those people were needed to help set things to rights."

Lady Derby gave a trill of laughter. "Oh, you are a knowing one, Miss Delacourt! Surely you don't expect me to believe you aren't perfectly aware of the boxing match today?"

"Oh, was that today?" Ginny bluffed. "And here I was so sure it was to happen tomorrow," she added with an airy wave of her hand.

"Did you hear that, Your Grace?" Lady Derby asked of the saturnine man by her side. "I can hardly credit it, but she believed it was to happen tomorrow!" Clearly she found something amusing about this pronouncement, as she went off into gales of laughter, but the lips of the strange man didn't so much as curve into a smile. He did, however, sit up a bit straighter and regard Ginny with a more avid interest.

Evidently this was an important man and as such was perhaps better informed than even Lady Derby. Ginny cast about for something to say that might elicit an illuminating response without exposing her total lack of real knowledge. This proved to be a most taxing endeavor, and the four of them sat in silence for what seemed to Ginny to be an agonizing length of time.

Finally, she hit on something suitable. "It is wrong. What they say . . . it is all quite wrong," she hedged.

"Oh?" Lady Derby asked with a knowing glance for her companion.

"Lord Crenshaw does not fight for my honor, as there is no need for it to be expunged. I am guilty of nothing more than speaking aloud my observations."

Lady Derby's companion tilted his head in interest, his gaze never leaving Ginny's face even as he leaned back to hide his expression in the shadow of Lady Derby's bonnet, an enormous contraption of green-glazed chipped straw adorned with a clutch of faux cherries at the brim. Ginny thought how very well matched the cherries were to Lady Derby's faux red lips, especially in contrast to her creamy white pelisse of soft wool with red braiding and frogs and very smart cloth boots, dyed red, as well. Ginny, in a pelisse of palest old rose and a bonnet devoid of any adornment but the wide green ribbon tied in a jaunty bow under her chin, felt a perfect dowd in comparison.

"If that is true, Miss Delacourt, I wonder that you have not spoken aloud your sprightly observations on the carriage race tomorrow or the balloon ascension the day after," Lady Derby mused openly. "If I were to speak aloud my observations, in just your so refreshing manner, I would say that it was most odd you were off to buy bride clothes when the fate of your marriage hangs so precariously on the outcome of something as uncertain as a boxing match."

Ginny, the breath frozen in her lungs, was saved the impossible task of formulating a reply by the sudden furor down the street. Huzzahs and shouts of "He's done it!" rang in the air, causing the horses all up and down Bond Street to become restive and whinny, adding to the near-thunderous roar of confusion.

If only she knew what it was he had done.

Chapter Fourteen

Anthony, pacing his rooms on Jermyn Street, wondered what he had done. If he had hoped to keep the boxing match from ever reaching Ginny's ears, all hope of that was lost. The hue and cry that rose to greet him as he stepped outside of Gentleman Jackson's Boxing Academy could be heard as far as Chester. Worse yet, the fact that he had engaged in a boxing match with his own valet would be the *on dit* of the season. As tempting as it was to whisk Ginny away to the country to keep her from ever learning the truth, they would never be able to return to London without some gudgeon putting a flea in her ear about the three tasks her husband was adjured to accomplish and from which he had fled.

There was nothing for it but to follow through on his promise to his uncle to the best of his ability. To that end, he called Conti into his presence with the intention of laying plans. He was expected at Wembley House in a matter of hours, and every minute counted.

"Conti, let us make matters clear between us. Your cousin . . ."

"Yes! I am Conti, but my mother was a Fagniani!"

"Yes," Anthony said through gritted teeth, casting about for a way to get through the conversation with the loquacious valet as quickly as possible. "Your cousin is the illegitimate daughter of the dancer known as Fagniani and the old Duke of Queensbury, is she not?"

"*Sì!* No! I shall explain. There are several claimants to her patronage, but Old Q left my cousin Maria a very large legacy een the case that he was her papa."

"So, Maria, your possible cousin, is sitting on the specialized carriage, the one of which I am in desperate need, of her possible father?"

"*Sì!* No! I shall explain. Maria, she ees my cousin, *sì!* She married the Earl of Yarmouth, but they did not like each other so well. Even before the Old Q died, she went to Paris and has lived there ever since."

"So . . . ," Anthony drawled. "The carriage is in London or in Paris?"

"No! *Sì!* My cousin, she ees een Paris. The carriage . . . ?" Conti shrugged his shoulders. "Who knows?"

Anthony folded his arms across his chest and narrowed his eyes at his so shortly ago brilliant but now utterly deranged valet. "So, you are suggesting I rap on the door of the Earl of Yarmouth, an acquaintance of mine, by the way, and request the use of a carriage that he might or might not have in his possession, that might or might not belong to his estranged wife, who might or might not have inherited it from someone who might or might not be her father?"

"*Sì!*" Conti exclaimed, throwing his hands into the air in triumph.

Anthony pressed his lips together and silently counted to ten, then ten again.

"Conti, this is *piu importante!* Do you know any of the servants in the earl's household?"

"*Ma certo!* When my cousin was a *bambina* with her *mama*, we used to laugh much together, but once she married and became a countess, I was allowed in only through the kitchen door."

"I see. And since her erstwhile flight to Paris?"

Anthony was amazed to see the look of pure abashment on Conti's face.

"*Sì*, I still go to the home of her husband. The old cook, she ees very good!"

Anthony raised his eyebrows. "By that I assume you refer to her cooking?"

"*Sì*, but what else?" Conti said with a shrug. "This English cooking ees no good. How else am I to fill out my fine clothing to perfection?"

"Then it is settled. You shall go at once to Yarmouth House in Regent's Park and get your hands on that carriage!"

"And eef the carriage is no more?"

"Then we shall have to make our escape in a balloon," Anthony said.

"What ees this? We are to travel in a balloon?"

"Not you and I, Conti, Miss Delacourt and I. Unless, of course, you know how to fly one," Anthony said with an ironic laugh.

"This, too, ees not beyond my power," Conti said with a bow.

Anthony rapped him on the back and bade him stand. "Conti, my man, you are a wonder! I shall endeavor to keep your genius under wraps, or Miss Delacourt might leave me for the better man."

"No, my lord, she sees none but you."

Anthony smiled at the sudden mist that rose in his eyes. "I do believe you are correct, as usual, Conti."

"You are a man that draws a woman's eye, my lord," Conti observed as he headed out the door to execute his orders.

"My thanks, Conti. I hadn't known you thought so highly of me."

"Eet is not the man, my lord, but the clothes on hees back!" Conti declared, just managing to close the door behind him before the volley of objects thrown by his master damaged his own finely turned-out ensemble.

With a sigh, Anthony turned to the mirror to inspect his appearance one last time before his departure for Wembley House. After the bout at Jackson's, Conti had insisted Anthony change his attire, something for which he could not fault the fastidious valet. In his dark blue coat, buff pantaloons, and that touch of lace at throat and wrist Ginny so loved, Anthony was pleased to admit he looked bang-up to the mark. What's more, the bruising on his knuckles was fading, and the boxing match with his valet had spared him any discoloration to the face. As he was disinclined to marry with a purple eye or bulbous nose, this was a circumstance wholly desired.

During the ride to Grosvenor Square he flirted with the idea of opening his budget to Ginny and telling her the whole. He knew she had learned of a boxing match and a wager from Lady Derby, but how much more of the story she was able to share with Ginny before he came on the scene at Almack's, he knew not.

How Lady Derby had learned of today's events was a more sizable mystery. What she intended to do with the information, had she the chance, was entirely predictable. Surely it would be better to tell Ginny the truth before she heard of it from someone who hadn't a care for her feelings. Yet he couldn't bear the thought of the blow to Ginny's happiness should she think for one moment their wedding might never come to pass.

Worse yet was his being lowered in Ginny's esteem once she learned of his feeble submission to his uncle's meddlesome demands. It would no doubt be much more comfortable to confess all once they were safely on their way to their wedding breakfast. Or, perhaps, after the honeymoon. Dash it all, if he made a clean breast of it following the birth of their firstborn, it would be none too soon!

By the time he arrived at Wembley House, he was on pins and needles. Keeping the truth from Ginny was one thing; staying silent when Grandmama knew all was another. Would she expect him to tell Ginny about the fight today and the carriage race tomorrow, or had Grandmama taken it upon herself to do so in his place? Making a mental note to keep her in the dark with regard to any plans for the days hence he had made or might ever make well into his uncertain future, he dashed up the front steps and rapped on the door.

He was greeted by a "Good evening" from Garner, the butler, a man who had known Anthony from his days in leading strings. Handing over his hat and gloves, he thought it wise to determine the mood of the ladies before climbing the stairs to the sitting room.

"So, how goes it today, old man?" he asked with a heartiness he did not feel. "Did the fitting for the wedding gown go well?"

"I cannot say, my lord," Garner said, placing the hat and gloves on the hall table. "It seemed there was the usual amount of loud, and might I add, execrable French being screeched at the top of Madame Badeau's lungs."

"I see," Anthony mused. "Dare I go up?"

"The so-called Frenchwoman has departed," Garner said as he headed up the stairs, signaling Anthony to follow. "However, Her Grace and the young miss seem a bit frayed about the edges."

"Is the frock not to her liking, then? Or was it something else she did not fancy?"

"Again, I cannot say. Only the words in French made their way below stairs, and I do not speak French, my lord. It is not a lack I feel the loss of," Garner patiently explained, his eyes suddenly moist.

As Garner's nephew was killed at the Battle of Vauchamps a year or so previous, Anthony could sympathize with the butler's tears as well as his intense dislike of all things French.

When they reached the white-paneled doors of the sitting room, Anthony dismissed the butler to his pantry, where it was common knowledge that a bottle of comfort was kept at hand for moments like these. "It's quite all right, Garner, you needn't announce me. I'll let myself in."

Wishing for a bit of a restorative himself and having none, Anthony resolutely pushed open the door. Despite his apprehension, the sight that greeted his eyes was wholly unexpected. Scattered about the room was a plethora of fabric, bows, and, unaccountably, feathers. Sitting in the midst of the disarray was Ginny, her usually well-pinned hair liberally sprinkled with drifts of downy detritus among the curls that had escaped their moorings to bewitchingly frame her face. Grandmama, whose once-famed beauty was never evident to Anthony, looked even less pleasing with a tiny feather clinging to the end of her pointy nose.

Feeling suddenly less at a disadvantage, he shut the door with a loud snap in hopes it would obliterate the sound of his unwarranted snigger.

"And how are my two roosting hens today?"

Ginny, whose previously vacant stare changed to seething anger at his words, turned to face him. "Oh! That is all that was wanted!" she cried, springing to her feet. Anthony noted that they were bare and her green-sprigged muslin gown seemed hastily donned.

"It would seem that Madame Badeau has only recently made her departure," he said with another visual tour of the room.

"So it would seem," Grandmama agreed, brushing the feather from her nose. "However, strange as it sounds, we have been sitting in just this manner for an absolute age." Sighing, she watched Ginny as she angrily hunted and plucked feathers from her hair with the aid of the mirror over the mantel. "I do not understand young ladies of this generation, Anthony. And I most certainly do not understand that woman who is making up Ginny's gown!"

"In that case, you have the advantage of me, Grandmama, as I understand nothing at all whatsoever."

"That is a categorical inaccuracy!" Ginny cried, whirling around, causing feathers to flit from her hair like embers from a fire. "Of all who are present, it is you who are omniscient!"

Anthony, at *point non plus* in spite of Ginny's claims, gazed at her in a puzzled amazement that quickly turned to appreciation. Gad, the girl's eyes were magnificent when she was angry! However, the fact that there was no clue to the question at hand to be found in her charmingly flushed face eventually made itself known, and he was forced to look elsewhere. The bits of muslin and lace scattered about the room seemed a good, albeit shocking, place to start.

"My darling, clearly something has gone terribly awry. Is it your gown? Do you not fancy it?" Whether or not the bits and pieces he was even now beholding was indeed her wedding attire was a question he, with some difficulty, abstained from asking.

"I adore it above all things," she said with a saucy lift of the chin. "But that is beside the point!"

Beginning to feel a bit ill-used, Anthony refrained from taking what could be deemed a menacing step toward his beloved. "Then can no one explain to me why the room looks like a giant game of spillikins and my betrothed like Ophelia?"

"How dare you allude to Shakespeare at such a moment!" Ginny cried, raising her hand as if to strike him, but Anthony deftly caught her wrist before any damage could be done. He'd be cursed if he were to be landed a blow after having gone to such lengths to avoid bruising earlier in the day.

"Sweetheart," he said, pulling her into his arms in spite of Grandmama's proximity, "forgive me. I regret my choice of words." His thoughts could not help but go to their time spent quarantined at the Barringtons', when they had each declared their love for the other using a mask of Shakespeare's devising. She had never told him how she felt about his appropriation of the character Caliban in the throes of passion for his Miranda, but he would never forget the moment when the shrewish Kate claimed him as her own. His heart expanded with the memory, and he determined that whatever it was that troubled her, he would make it right.

"I shall collar that modiste and fetch her here this very moment," he said, wanting with every fiber of his soul to protect

Ginny against error, endangerment, and English seamstresses who impersonated the French. He patted her on the back and waited for the sobs to subside until, gradually, he realized there were no tears at all whatsoever and his beloved was standing as stiff as a statue against his chest.

Maneuvering her gently away by the shoulders, he took a step back to look into her face, but she would not meet his eyes. Cut to the quick, he dropped his arms and turned away, unable to look upon her pain a moment longer.

"Grandmama? Do you have anything to say to this?"

She shrugged. "Only that there was an argument. I daresay Madame Badeau is halfway to Hertfordshire by now."

"Grandmama, how could you?" Anthony retorted. "It is Ginny's happiness you have squandered with your dislikes and sharp tongue!"

"It is not I who drove the woman away," she said with a reluctant air.

Quickly, he glanced up and caught Ginny's expression in the fireplace mirror just as her face drained of all color.

Making a show of regarding his fingernails, he asked a question, the answer to which he felt would shed the most light on the perplexing situation. "And that mess on the floor? Tell me that is not the gown my bride is to wear the day we are to wed?"

With his words, Ginny came immediately to life. "No, it is not! She has taken that with her, and I wish her joy of it!" she cried, rushing from the room.

Although frustrated by her demeanor, Anthony felt a surge of relief to know that his betrothed had not torn to shreds the gown that symbolized their impending union. Surveying the ruin on the floor through his quizzing glass, he contemplated his next question. He knew his grandmama must be far past distressed and suspected she had the wherewithal to answer only one question further. He knew he must choose wisely.

"Pray tell, from whence came the feathers?"

Grandmama threw her hands in the air. "Ginny is fit to be tied, and you ask about feathers?"

"Oddly enough, I feel they are at the crux of the matter. Perhaps they were meant to be adhered to the gown, a thought that makes me shudder. I can only assume it should have angered Ginny to no end should the modiste have insisted upon them. It would explain much and would allow me to safely blame Ginny's anger on the natural anxiety any woman might feel when she is about to be wed."

"No," Grandmama said, folding her hands primly in her lap. "That is not what happened."

"Ah! Well, perhaps Madame Badeau had some other suggestion to which Ginny took exception, whereupon she speared a pillow with a pair of scissors and scattered its feathers about the room."

"No, Ginny was already in a taking before Madame Badeau arrived. In fact, we have been at daggers drawn all afternoon."

"Very well, then, Grandmama, if you are not going to tell me what this is about, I shall take myself off."

"Oh, Anthony, you must know I would tell you if I knew! All I can say is that Ginny has been out of sorts most of the day, that she gave the modiste such a difficult time and, indeed, was so relentlessly free with her less than flattering observations that Madame Badeau became incensed. She ripped open a cushion and poured the contents over Ginny's head, upon which that madwoman snatched up the dress and ran screaming from the house!"

Anthony felt the stirrings of a wild hope beat in his heart. "You say Ginny was relentless?"

"Well, yes, she was."

He tapped the quizzing glass against his lips and pondered. "You say she was less than flattering?"

"Never more so!" Grandmama averred.

He pursed his lips and regarded her out of the corner of his eye. "Yet she claims to love the gown. This can mean only one thing. She is back! My adorable shrew has resurfaced!"

"Indeed, I think you could be correct," Grandmama said slowly. "Perhaps the strain was becoming too much for her. She has seemed oddly subdued as of late."

"I must admit," he said as he began to pace the room, "I appreciate her more courtly manner when in company, but, oh, how I have missed her! I have even wondered if perhaps her restrained behavior has been born of a love for the role of duchess more than her love for me." A burden he hadn't realized was in existence lifted from his shoulders, leaving him to feel lighter than the feathers that littered every surface of the room. "And here I thought perhaps she had run into Lady Derby and gotten wind of my uncle's demands. Leave it to him to make matters seem worse than they are already."

Suddenly, darkness intruded into his thoughts, and his pacing came to an abrupt stop. "Grandmama, you haven't told Ginny of the boxing match? Or the race? And, gad, not the balloon?"

"Of course not! I have no more wish to see her hurt than do you, nor more anxious than she is already! But you must be less cowardly than I and tell her the truth. I daresay she feels you are hiding something from her, and it is causing her to feel peevish and quarrelsome."

"In two days' time it will no longer matter," he said with an airy wave of his hand, and he quit the room without so much as a "Good night." Once in the hall, however, he felt less sure of himself. Stopping at the bottom of the staircase that led up to the bedchamber where Ginny was wont to flee, he was all at once filled with a longing to tell her everything. Surely the hurt she would feel for the truth would be nothing compared to the hurt she already knew. He stood unmoving, willing her to appear, for what seemed an uncommonly long time. However, she did not come, and he was forced to collect his hat and gloves and depart. Conti would be waiting.

Chapter Fifteen

Ginny couldn't begin to fathom why she had come; carriage races had never interested her in the past. Besides which, she was sure to be treated to some loathsome snub à la Lady Derby. Nevertheless, she had come, and if forced to answer why, she would say it was to please Grandaunt Regina. Her formidable guardian had been so unlike herself of late, tender and even tremulous at times. When Ginny had crept into Grandaunt's room the night previous to beg her pardon for her untenable behavior, the old woman was so overcome, Ginny feared there would be actual tears.

"Why, Grandaunt!" she said, aghast. "Whatever is the matter?" she asked, daring to seat herself on the edge of the dowager duchess' bed. It was adorned with quantities of antique lace and was very fine, but it was her grandaunt's standoffish demeanor that had kept Ginny from becoming so familiar in the past. "Everything will be all right in the end."

Grandaunt rallied with a frown. "You mean to say you are not angry with him?"

"Yes, of course I am!" Ginny answered. "But my anger in no way lessens my love for him. I intend to marry him, and marry him I shall, if there are only the rags in the parlor remaining in which to do so."

When the expected discourse on how a future duchess does not marry in rags was not forthcoming, Ginny became a bit alarmed. "Grandaunt, there is something you are not saying." She stood and turned away so her grandaunt would not see the tears that had sprung to her eyes. "There is something Anthony is not saying, as well."

"You are most correct, Ginerva," Grandaunt said in a voice more like her own. "But I have given my word I would not be the one to enlighten you. However, if you were to go out with me in the carriage tomorrow for a jaunt to Hyde Park, I am persuaded explanations will be wholly unnecessary."

Ginny knew it was Lady Derby's rumored carriage race to which Grandaunt referred and hesitated to agree to the outing. She did not know if she wished to see Anthony just yet; however, the possibility of disappointing Grandaunt again so soon was a circumstance beyond bearing. Without either woman revealing what she knew about the carriage race, plans were made to sally forth to Hyde Park shortly before luncheon on the morrow.

Nevertheless, once she had returned to her own bed, Ginny felt some misgivings. She knew Anthony did not want her to know of the race—knew, too, that he would be angry with Grandaunt for letting the cat out of the bag. What's more, she was ashamed. Could he still love her after the way she had behaved? What if he turned from her in hatred or, worse yet, utter indifference? The lingering anger she felt for his concealment of the threat to their future all but evaporated in the fear she felt at the possible loss of his love and regard.

And what of Lady Derby? Ginny was unsure she would be inclined to hold her tongue if faced with the usual barbs from Anthony's former betrothed. The carriage race was sure to be as well attended as the boxing match. Should Ginny insult Lady Derby in return, it would be under the watchful eye of Society. And then there was the betting book at White's to regard with misery. No doubt there were pages and pages of wagers betting against Anthony's triumph. Though she knew he would marry her regardless of what anyone said, Society at large would be privy only to what Lady Derby had made sure to spread about.

Now that she and Grandaunt were at Hyde Park, there was no turning back. The teeming mass of carriages all jostling for position along the Serpentine Road prevented them from moving an inch. Because the fashionable hour to see and be seen at the barrier to the park was four o'clock in the afternoon, the race had been planned for an early hour so as disrupt as few pleasure-seekers as possible. Yet, as she gazed about her, Ginny was persuaded she had never seen such a crush in the park at any hour of the day. Whether or not Lady Derby was among them, Ginny was too nervous to ascertain. The thought of encountering her made Ginny feel slightly ill, and she kept her gaze mostly in her lap or on the ground before her so as not to mistakenly fall under Lady Derby's notice.

"Well!" Grandaunt exclaimed. "If this race does not commence immediately, we shall be brown as figs!"

Ginny's constant surveillance of the road where the race was to be held had so far yielded no clues that a race was to occur at all. "I can see that Anthony has not arrived, but what of his opponent? Is he here?"

Grandaunt shook her head. "You do not properly apprehend the situation, my dear. Anthony is to race against time, not an actual opponent. The fastest time to be achieved by anyone is slightly more than nineteen miles per hour in a chaise and four; therefore, he will need to do the nineteen miles in less than fifty-nine minutes. It is quite impossible! The record has been held for over fifty years. Meanwhile, where is he? I have no desire to be pinned like a butterfly under glass a moment longer than need be."

"Nineteen miles?" Ginny exclaimed. "He will be out of view within a few minutes' time. Why are so many people gathered to watch an event that will go mostly unseen?"

"Allow me to explain," came a familiar voice from the carriage to their left.

It was Lord Avery, a wholly disagreeable circumstance, as it could only mean that Lucinda was not far off. Ginny supposed Grandaunt would utter the usual greeting, but the old dame looked as if she had just swallowed a fly. Ginny realized it would be up to her to do the pretty. She peered into the neighboring carriage and saw that Lucinda was indeed in attendance. "How good of you to enlighten us, my lord, and good day to you, Lady Avery," she said with a sinking heart, knowing it would be bellows to mend from here on out.

"Oooooh, Ginny, you must be in raptures!" Lucinda said with a squeal. "Lord Crenshaw is to duel on horseback for your honor! I have made Eustace promise he will do the same for me one day, only he must wear a blindfold to make it even more spectacular!"

"My flower," Lord Avery interjected, "as I have explained more than thrice, he is not to duel, nor will he be on horseback. There will be horses, yes, but it is merely a race."

"A race?" Lucinda screeched. "You mean to say there will be no shooting? What is romantical about a mere race? You have dragged me from my comfortable chaise to watch a carriage race?" she cried, pummeling the velvet collar of her husband's powder-blue coat with a rapid volley of her tiny fists.

Lord Avery sighed and attempted a smile. "That is not precisely what happened, dearest." Ginny could smell the sharp burst of perspiration that was beading his brow; it was clear that marriage to Lucinda was beginning to pall a bit. "As I recall, my flower, I insisted you should stay home and rest up from whatever indisposition it is that ails you today, while I came here on my own."

Lucinda sniffed and leaned back, waving her handkerchief in front of her face. "I should never have come! The heat is unendurable, and the flies . . . ! Why, I have never been subjected to such a large quantity of the horrid things in my entire life!

Ginny," she said, leaning over the side of the carriage to afford herself a better view, "you couldn't possibly mind should I swat them all your way, as you are from the country. I am persuaded girls from the country are well-conversant with flies."

As Lucinda had only very recently altered her place of residence to town from the very same countryside from which Ginny hailed, any number of hot words sprang to Ginny's tongue. However, it would seem that the choleric dowager duchess had a few home truths of her own for Lucinda.

"I should say not, you guileless nincompoop!" Grandaunt Regina said with a roll of her eyes. "Neither Ginerva nor I have any more reason to endure flies than do you, Lady Avery. However, where there are horses, there are flies. It behooves a lady to endure them, as well as many an indisposition, in courageous silence!"

Lucinda's pretty brow furrowed in bewilderment, and she said nothing for a blessedly long moment. It occurred to Ginny that Lucinda was incapable of speaking and thinking at the same time. Sadly, exactly which phrase or utterance might cause Lucinda to buckle down to the task of thoughtful silence was anybody's guess. As the silence grew, Ginny and Lord Avery exchanged a knowing glance that held for a moment until it skittered away in self-conscious guilt.

In the end it was Lord Avery who, with a heavy sigh, bravely threw himself into the breach. "As I was saying, dear ladies, allow me to explain. Lord Crenshaw has elected to run a race against time. It has been agreed upon that he will begin here at the west end of the Serpentine Road. When he reaches the end, he will turn north on Park Lane, then west on North Carriage Drive, south on West Carriage Drive, then east on South Carriage Drive until he arrives at the corner and turns northwest onto the Serpentine, where he will arrive just where he began."

"Pray tell, how long will that take?" Ginny asked, mindful of the dowager's aversion to the sun.

"Only a bit more than seven minutes, if my math skills are correct, though numbers were never my strong suit. Words have been, and ever will be, the only food for my soul," Lord Avery admitted with an almost girlish bat of his lashes.

"And *moi*, Eustace!" Lucinda insisted. "Do you not recollect the time you wrote that lovely poem in which *I* was food for your soul? Oh, it was so romantic, Ginny, you would never credit it! Everything about me was edible."

Ginny thought the concept was entirely creditable but was prevented from saying so, as Lucinda never so much as paused for a gasp of air.

"My lips were cherries, my eyes were blueberries, my hair was spun wheat, and so on and so forth," she added in an uncharacteristic attempt at getting to the point as quickly as possible. "In the end, he ate me all up, even though I must say, some of it sounded rather nasty. Eustace says we shall all be food for worms one day, but I daresay the mention of it in this particular poem made the whole thing a sight less delicious than it could have been."

"Yes, of course," Lord Avery hastily interjected.

Ginny was ready with a hasty interjection of her own. "But I thought the whole point of the race was to beat the time of nineteen miles in under an hour. How is that to be accomplished if the distance around the park requires only seven minutes to run?"

"A very good question, Miss Delacourt! He shall be required to run the carriage along the Serpentine Road and around the entire park eight times in order to be able to say he raced the full nineteen miles."

"Eight times! Oh, Eustace, I fear I shall go into a decline before then!"

Secretly, Ginny echoed Lucinda's dismay but held her tongue.

"It shall all be quite exciting," Grandaunt said with uncommon glee. "We shall see him pass us by many times before the end of the race, and he shall hear us cheering him along!"

Miss Delacourt Has Her Day

Ginny wasn't sure if a cheer was in order, when, just then, the carriage hove into view.

"What is wrong with it? It looks as if it has all been burned up!" Lucinda cried.

"Not burned. Taken apart piece by piece!" Lord Avery cried. "Deuce take it, I should not have bet against the man! He has this race all sewn up, and the rest of us none the wiser."

In growing delight, Ginny took in the sight of the carriage, stripped of most of its parts. There were no doors, side panels, seating, squabs, or roof, only the framework, a place for the driver to repose, the wheel equipage, and the tracings for the horses, of which there were four. Instantly she understood that the lack of adornment of any kind would make short work for the horses, lending wings to their hooves.

Grandaunt let out a bark of laughter. "You are quite right, my lord. Oh, that Old Q was a canny one! I doubt not that this is the very carriage the Duke of Queensbury had built especially for his infamous race, one that was run . . . Well! I was no more than a babe at the time."

Lord Avery gasped. "You don't say! The very one? Why, who even knew it still existed? The man is a master!"

"Eustace," Lucinda said, a formidable pout blooming on her face. "You have never called *me* a master. I think I should like it if you called me that."

"But, my darling, of what could I possibly deem you a master?"

"Well, I could be the Master of She Who Loves Poetry. Or perhaps the Master of Domestic Bliss," Lucinda suggested.

"Yes, but, my heart, you are not a man."

"Of course I am not a man, Eustace! What a faradiddle!"

"I think what Lord Avery is trying to say, Lady Avery, is that you could never be a *master*. You will always be a *mistress*," Ginny explained.

"A mistress? Why, I have never been a mistress in my life! Eustace," Lucinda said, clutching at her husband's arm. "Am I a mistress? I think not, for I was there at the wedding, and I am persuaded that we are man and wife!"

Grandaunt uttered a groan, prompting Ginny to take the old woman's hand and give it a squeeze. "It shall all be over soon, dearest," she said.

"Not soon enough! If that boy does not jump into that so-called carriage this instant and run the race in less than fifty-nine minutes, I declare I shall disown him!"

As if warned from above, Anthony immediately strode out onto the road. He studiously ignored the crowd and busied himself with the task of checking the horses and carriage. Only once did he lift his head, causing Ginny to feel a frisson of delight when his eyes went directly to her face. It was if he knew precisely where to find her from the moment he came into view. He held her gaze with his own for what seemed a scandalously excessive length of time, but he did not smile or say a word. It wasn't until he had turned away and climbed nimbly onto his seat that, she realized, nor had she.

"I feel that he is angry with me," Ginny said for Grandaunt's ears only.

"You must be blind, child. That look he gave you would melt ice! The boy is clearly heels-over-head in love, and if he can get himself together in time to win this race, I will be hornswoggled!"

Privately, Ginny thought he looked very much together, indeed. He wore a bottle-green corded jacket over a mace-and-nutmeg waistcoat and dark serge pantaloons paired with gold-tasseled Hessians and York Tan gloves. As his head was bare, she was treated to the sight of his dark curls glowing in the sun. Ginny could only assume that his lack of headgear meant he intended to travel at speeds too high for the retention of a hat. As he took the reins in his hands and prepared himself for the signal to proceed, the excitement in the air became palpable.

A man stepped into the road and held aloft his pocket watch.

"That is so we know he shall be timing the race," Lucinda supplied.

"Why, Lady Avery," Grandaunt mused, "it would seem there is more going on in that head of yours than one supposed."

"How very kind of you!" Lucinda said with a clap of her hands.

Ginny was persuaded that Grandaunt's remark was downright charitable, but she had little time to reflect on Lucinda's mush-for-brains, for just then the man with the watch waved a small flag, and the carriage lurched into motion.

All in all, the race was a good deal more exciting than Ginny had anticipated. Grandaunt had been correct in that it was above all things exhilarating to watch the carriage heave into view after each journey around the makeshift track. The prodigious amount of dust kicked up by the hooves of four horses was another matter entirely. It rose in great clouds such that it was a wonder Anthony could see well enough to follow the road. Clustered so close to the track as they were, a number of carriage occupants were affrighted by the proximity of Anthony's large wheels to their own as he spun by. As a result, there was much gasping in awe as well as for breath when the clouds of dust threatened to choke the spectators.

Once the lightning-fast carriage had spun by, and the cheers, as well as the inevitable boos from those who had bet against a win, had died away, and the dust on the road had cleared, the company at large entertained themselves by various means. For Ginny and Grandaunt this meant being subjected to Lucinda's endless inane chatter, something from which Ginny was somewhat saved by virtue of watching the group of children in the carriage parked to the far side of the Averys. There were two girls and a boy, all of whom pranced from the carriage the moment their mother deemed it safe. As a result, they could regularly be found wandering the row of carriages, plucking flowers and weeds alike and encouraging the gift of sweetmeats from other carriage occupants with their round-cheeked smiles.

Ginny found the girls to be lovely, but it was the boy, the youngest of the group, who most caught her eye. He toddled along behind his sisters in rapt adoration, and Ginny wondered how much less lonely her childhood might have been had she a brother or sister with whom to play. She would have taken great care of a younger sibling, just as did these girls, who kept a wary eye out for the racing carriage, making sure to round up their little brother and return him to the safety of their mother's arms before he could be mowed down by the horses.

Ginny made a game of observing them. How many people importuned for candy in exchange for bundles of wildflowers would fall under the children's bright-eyed spell this time around? The number seemed to grow with each of Anthony's turns around the track, and Ginny could only mourn her lack of comestibles, as it broke her heart to turn the children away again and again.

In spite of the fun, Ginny spent a great deal of time mentally wringing her hands in anxiety over their antics. The little boy was highly inclined to dash across the road altogether and clamber through the brush that divided the Serpentine Road from the parallel river in order to splash a bit in the water. His sisters dragged him back on a regular basis, but it wasn't long before Ginny began to worry that the children might not make it back across the road in time to elude the carriage. At the speed Anthony was going and the quantity of dust that obscured his view, she feared he would not be able to stop soon enough should the children not clear the road in time.

At long last the carriage was about to come around the bend for the last time, and Ginny's current trials would cease: Lucinda's chatter, her anxiety for the children, and the race itself, on the result of which the fate of her marriage was rumored to rest. Ginny wondered, not for the first time, what had instigated the need for these athletic contests, but she fully comprehended how things stood with Society. Someone, doubtless Lady Derby and her entourage, had put it about that Anthony must perform certain tasks in order to marry Ginny. Once word was out and wagers made for and against, Ginny understood that Anthony had little choice but to proceed regardless of the utter lack of veracity in every word. Who could possibly be so insensible as to deny them marriage based on whether or not he won a carriage race? The idea was preposterous, and her only sorrow in the entire proceedings was Anthony's lack in confiding in her the truth.

Suddenly the cloud of dust that inevitably preceded the carriage rose into the air, and the reasons behind the need for these contests meant little more to Ginny than the dandelions that dotted the grass. The excitement in the air was growing with the cries and shouts of the spectators, who were jumping from their conveyances and standing in such large clusters that it impeded Ginny's view of the proceedings.

"Ginerva, do stand and see what is happening!" Grandaunt insisted. "With all this noise it will be a wonder if we will hear that little man with the watch call the time."

Ginny was only too glad to rise to her feet just in time to see Anthony's chaise and four round the bend, then come to a screeching halt only a few yards shy of the finish line. The man with the flag became extremely agitated and ran to the carriage through a colossal cloud of dust, waving his arms and shouting that Anthony had stopped too soon, but Anthony, his face caked with dirt, either did not hear or cared not. Jumping out of the carriage from the side opposite his audience, he ran through the bit of brush and scree at the river's edge and dashed into the water, while the crowd roared in disbelief.

"What is it?" Grandaunt asked with a tug at Ginny's skirts.

"I don't know exactly, but he is every inch covered in dust. It looks for all the world that it has driven him mad, as he has run into the river and is splashing about in a craze!"

"Oh, look!" Lucinda cried as she jumped up and down in

her carriage, causing all the nearby horses to whicker and neigh. "He has found a dolly in the water!"

Ginny was aghast to see that Lucinda was correct, or mostly. It did seem at first that the object Anthony carried in his arms was a doll, as it had a head and four limbs. However, it also had round pink cheeks and bore a clutch of dandelions in its hand.

"No! Oh, no, it's him, that precious little boy!" Ginny clambered down from the carriage unassisted and pushed her way through the crowd that had gathered between her and her objective just as a sharp cry from the boy's mother rose above the gasps of dismay. Once clear of the crowd, she ran to Anthony with outstretched arms to receive the wet and muddy bundle he unhesitatingly deposited into her care.

"He'll be all right. Find his mother."

"Yes, but . . . how did you—?" Ginny asked, searching his eyes made even more blue through the streaks of wet dust that cascaded from his hair and down his face.

"I saw him fall in just before I rounded the bend. I stopped as soon as I possibly could!"

Speechless, Ginny was saved from forming a reply, for the little boy's mother appeared to scoop him from her arms, prompting the child to wail his fear now that he was safe in the circle of his mother's love.

Without another glance Anthony dashed back to the carriage and vaulted onto the seat. Taking the reins in his hands, he whipped the horses into movement and drove the few yards to the finish line as delineated by the man with the watch and the flag, who once again waved it and pronounced the race complete.

"He has won!" shouted the man with the flag as Anthony made his way out of the carriage. "He has beat the best time for a carriage race by a full minute!" he cried, and, grabbing Anthony's wrist, he thrust his arm high above his head.

In spite of the fact that most men in attendance had doubtless wagered against a win, huzzahs filled the air. So loud was the cheering that the whimpering of the little boy was entirely drowned out, and more than one hat was tossed into the sky to land on the road at Anthony's feet. Ginny was surprised to see that among the curly-rimmed beavers, half-moon bicornes, and hunting hats, more than a few high-poke bonnets could be seen littering the road.

The mood was festive indeed, and it was time to find Grandaunt. However, Ginny took a moment to speak with the boy's mother, who still stood by her side.

"Is he going to be all right?" she asked.

"Yes," the mother replied with a grateful smile. "He is a naughty little thing, and it is not, I am sad to say, his first tumble into the water. I should have been paying him more mind."

Secretly, Ginny agreed, but she could hardly say so. Noting that full color had returned to the boy's cheek, she gave it a buss and began to look about her for a clear path back to her conveyance, when a shrill voice from above broke through the noisy confusion.

"Hold! Might His Grace have your attention, please?" came the voice as if from thin air. Ginny looked above her head and spotted the disagreeable Mr. Simmons, confrere of Lady Derby, high in the branches of a tree.

"His Grace has something of import to announce!" Mr. Simmons claimed, and he directed the attention of all in attendance to a man standing in a carriage near the last bend in the road around which Anthony had just come. Ginny noted that it was the man who had been in the carriage with Lady Derby the day prior.

"There has been a mistake!" he shouted. "The race has been lost! The time was two minutes over, not one under!"

There came a murmuring from the crowd, but it would

seem there were few who were willing to counter His Grace. Ginny turned to see Anthony's reaction, but he was deep in conversation with the man who had officiated the proceedings. Together they nodded, whereupon Anthony climbed to stand precariously on the seat of the denuded carriage and turned to face his opponent.

"Mr. Shirley informs me he has timed the race accurately!" he shouted loudly enough to be heard by all. "He also timed the disruption and subtracted the minutes lost from the overall time, bringing the race time to just under fifty-eight minutes!"

His Grace made a loud *tsk* that seemed to echo and reverberate in the hushed silence that now prevailed. "And what of Mr. Shirley's timepiece? An ordinary watch has not the delicacy of function to accurately record such infinitesimal periods of time!"

"By that I suppose I am to assume that yours does, Your Grace. However, Mr. Shirley's timepiece is no ordinary pocket watch. It is, in fact, a chronograph and is capable of telling time with the greatest accuracy as well as stopping it."

Gasps of dismay or surprise, Ginny was uncertain which, rose from every direction, quickly followed by shouts along the lines of, "Give the man Mr. Shirley's time!" as well as, "I am with His Grace!" When two men in uncomfortably close proximity to Ginny looked as if they would come to blows over their differing viewpoints, she began to feel a bit alarmed. Before she had a moment to reflect on how she was to get through the mob to the relative safety of her carriage, Anthony materialized at her side, his arm around her waist, pushing their way through the crowd. He smelled of dirt, perspiration, a fair amount of horse, and, unaccountably, eau de cologne. She had never known any combination to smell lovelier.

Sensing that he would soon be off again the moment they reached their objective, Ginny considered pelting him with questions, but it would seem that she had her own to answer first.

"How fares the boy?" he asked. Circling her waist with his hands, he lifted her into the carriage, leaving Ginny to think what a pity it was that men's fashions did not lean toward the display of bare arms, of what would seem, in this case, to be the superbly well-muscled variety.

"He's fine," she said once she had caught her breath after the unexpected ride through the air. "His mother is ever so grateful!"

"And your gown? Is it still on holiday in Hertfordshire?"

"We have seen or heard nothing of Madame Badeau since I saw you last."

He nodded his understanding but avoided looking her in the eye, almost as if he were ashamed or afraid of being caught out in a lie. Once he saw she was safely settled, he turned his attention to Grandaunt Regina. "Good afternoon, Grandmama," he said with his usual aplomb, though his gaze was focused on His Grace, who was still standing in his carriage a few yards down the row.

Grandaunt lost no time in making her wishes known. "Anthony, don't let that man get the best of you! Tell him your grandmother insists that you beat Old Q's time! And you saved the life of that poor little mite. Well done, my boy, well done!" she added, her eyes glowing with pride.

However, he had melted into the crowd before he could see her pleasure in his accomplishments. Ginny could only assume he had gone off to do his grandmother's bidding. But who was "that man"? He was styled "His Grace," which meant he could only be a duke. Anthony's uncle was said to be about to breathe his last at any moment. Common sense dictated it could not be he.

"Whoever this man is, he must have bet a great sum against Anthony's winning the race. He could have no other reason to cause such a commotion."

Grandaunt sighed. "Ever since Anthony's grandfather departed this life, there has been only that man left to cut up my peace."

Ginny felt her eyes go wide. "But no! It cannot be!"

"Indeed it can. He is my son, the Duke of Marcross."

Chapter Sixteen

As Anthony pushed his way through the crowd to confront his uncle, the duke, he indulged himself in an examination of his feelings. He was a bit taken aback to learn he felt nothing if not unworthy: of Ginny's love, of her admiration, and, most of all, her forgiveness. Refraining from telling Ginny of the three trials his uncle had insisted upon was hardly better than telling her an outright lie.

What's more, he had insisted upon Grandmama's connivance in the matter. What dark thoughts must have gone through Ginny's mind when she found herself an unwitting spectator of a race run by the man she trusted above all others, he shuddered to learn. How utterly frivolous the whole event must have seemed in her eyes, especially in light of their impending union and her missing wedding gown. How he wished he had spoken to her of this whole harebrained scheme of his uncle's as well as his own reasons for participating in it.

He had fully expected her to be as angry as she had been the night previous, yet she had put aside her feelings of betrayal in order to cheer him on. She had come to him, unbidden, when he needed her help in finding the family of that poor, half-drowned scamp. Indeed, she had praised him for what any man might have done had he the knowledge and opportunity.

If he had lost one iota of Ginny's love and respect through

the events of this day, there would be no end to his need to blame himself. Yet, as he pushed his way ever closer to the duke, it occurred to him that there was more than enough blame to be assigned all around. His uncle topped the list, but the names of Lady Derby and Mr. Simmons came immediately to mind, as well. If they hadn't spread about the news and made a wager-worthy spectacle of both the boxing match and the race, there was a chance no one would have been the wiser. Barring that, he might have consigned the whole thing to perdition without fear that Ginny, some months or years hence, would learn how her husband had turned tail and fled rather than fight for his uncle's approval.

By the time he came face-to-face with the threesome seated in the carriage—they who had quite possibly dashed all of his hopes and dreams and, worse yet, Ginny's—he was too vexed to wonder what miracle had been wrought that had allowed his uncle to rise from his deathbed.

"Have you done amusing yourself by meddling in my life, Uncle?"

"Why, Crenshaw, you look a bit worse for wear. I had thought it quite impossible I should find you looking a mite less than exquisite in what remains of my lifetime, but there it is," the duke said with a sniff.

Remembering himself, Anthony sketched a bow to both Lady Derby and Mr. Simmons, allowing himself time to weigh his response with care. "I am in possession of a valet who would mourn as do you should he be here to see me. Instead of being in attendance today to watch the clothing he so tenderly cares for become grimed in dust, sweat, and the tears of one *enfant* in particular, not to mention the befouled waters of the Serpentine, he is off procuring a balloon." He paused and favored his uncle with a knowing smile. "Shall I ride after him, hell for leather, and inform him that this particular service is no longer required?"

Lady Derby's shriek of laughter at this utterance could

doubtless be heard at the far end of Hyde Park, while Mr. Simmons' goggle-eyed stare was a wonder to behold. The duke, however, merely frowned and narrowed his eyes.

"I do believe we had an agreement, Crenshaw. You were to perform three tasks, as specified and to my satisfaction. In return I would pronounce my blessing upon your marriage to a certain Miss Delacourt."

"Very well, then," Anthony conceded. "I shall safely assume the first two tasks have been performed to your satisfaction and will proceed with the balloon ascension tomorrow morning as planned."

"The boxing match was craftily done, and I commend you, Crenshaw. I have little respect for the opinion of the outcome of today's race, but it would seem I am outnumbered there. I shall concede two wins and look forward to the balloon ascension with every degree of anticipation. However, the terms of the agreement state that you need to fly the balloon, on your own, from one location to the other. Where do you intend to go up, and where do you intend to put down the balloon?" the duke queried.

Anthony knew that the place of departure was already known to all and sundry, particularly those who availed themselves of the information in the betting book at White's. He could only hope Regent's Park would be a deal less crowded than Hyde was today. However, the place of landing was one piece of information Anthony loathed to divulge for reasons he planned to keep to himself until the last possible moment. As it was, there were too many eager ears about.

"I'm persuaded you are well aware of the location of my departure, sir. As to the landing, I will do you one better!" Anthony said with an airy wave of his hand that sent dust skittering across the lap of Lady Derby's cossack-green *gros de naples* gown, which was very fine but sadly at odds with the brick-red grogram ribbon that adorned her hat, an already hideous affair by virtue of its ridiculously high poke graced by a spray of what looked to be roadside weeds dangling over the brim. "I shall write the location on a piece of paper, in my own hand and sealed with my own signet, and leave it to the care of my grandmama. In days hence, there shall be none to claim they heard me say I had always meant to fly only as far as Harrow Road when you have evidence proclaiming it was my full intention to alight in Hampstead Heath all along."

"And when shall I be in possession of this paper?" the duke asked with a dubious air.

"Oh, you shall have it soon enough, never fear!" Anthony replied, examining his woefully dirty cuffs. As he planned to ensure that Grandmama, along with the precious paper, would be well on her way to Dunsmere by then, he trusted the duke would not learn of its contents until it was very much too late for him to make himself disagreeable. "Shall we shake on it, then, Your Grace?" Anthony asked, stripping off a filthy, wet glove and thrusting his hand under his uncle's nose.

"Hold a moment!" the duke said, recoiling from the dirt or the agreement, Anthony couldn't say which. "You haven't forgotten our arrangement with regards to Miss Delacourt's fate should you fail to land on target?"

"I would hardly call us in accord along those lines, Uncle!" Anthony said, hoping his heart hadn't visibly jumped from his chest. "If I were to fail in my endeavor, Miss Delacourt will yet remain in the capable guardianship of her Grandaunt Regina."

"I need not remind you, Crenshaw, that I am the head of her grandaunt's family, and if I see fit to pack your girl off to the country to marry Simmons' father, here, a widower with several brats get off his second wife still littering the house, then pack her off I shall!"

Anthony quelled the shudder of revulsion he felt at the thought of Ginny clutched in the grip of an older version of Simmons. Though he would never allow Ginny to fall into such a horrid marriage, he wasn't as sure of his valet's ability to fly a balloon. Anthony could only pray that, wherever they landed, there would be nobody about to bear witness to his uncle. As long as he was praying, he might as well add a bit about spiriting Ginny away and out of the power of men such as his uncle and his hoary widowers standing in the wings.

"Dearest Uncle, it would seem you are the crafty one! In exchange, if I should triumph, you must promise that after we are wed, you shall brook no argument and allow us to live our lives according to our own desires and wishes without this constant interference."

"Yes, I do believe I can go along with that, but only because your Miss Delacourt has a good deal of spirit. Indeed, she has bottom! Though I would rather see her wed to Mr. Simmons Senior, I shall enjoy watching her lead you a merry dance through life, if it comes to that."

"And you, sir? Have you put off your date with the devil long enough to witness such dancing?"

"I must say, I do feel a sight better than I have for years," the duke said, thumping his narrow chest with one fist. "However, one can never say for sure which way the wind might blow!"

"True," Anthony said, affecting not to notice how his uncle's free hand came to rest on Lady Derby's knee. "But should one read the signs aright, one might hazard a notion," he added with an arch of one eyebrow.

The duke frowned but did not remove his hand from its proprietary position. "Let us hope that the wind blows in just the right direction for you tomorrow." With that the duke took up the reins, whipped up the horses, and drove off into the dwindling crowd.

Anthony turned and walked back to where he had left Ginny and Grandmama. The row of carriages had mostly broken up and driven off, affording him a clear view of his beloved as she sat and patiently waited. He could not help but reflect on how her demure beauty outshone Lady Derby's exotic attractions in every way. While the former's costume had been loud, Ginny's gown of white spotted muslin under an old rose poplin spencer hit just the right note, while the bonnet of chip straw lined with white lace, adorned by one or two silk rosebuds and tied fetchingly under her chin, allowed her glossy chestnut curls to come alive.

When she spotted his approach and smiled her delight, his heart turned over in his chest. It occurred to him how this would be an opportune time to reveal the entire truth about his three tasks, yet it seemed impossible to speak of it so soon after his uncle's threats to marry her off to an ancient widower should Anthony fail in the execution of the duke's last injunction. After tomorrow, there would be more than enough time to tell her all.

"What did that unruly son of mine have to say, Anthony?" Grandmama asked the moment he drew near enough to hear her words.

"He has seen the error of his ways," he replied, wiping his hand clean on his handkerchief, as he had no wish to dirty Ginny's soft white glove with his kiss. "Demme, I have soiled it after all!" he said upon inspecting the result.

Ginny surveyed his handiwork, as well, and, laughing, proclaimed it perfect. "I shall cherish this glove forever, as it bears the mark of your love in the exact replica of your lips!"

Suddenly, for Anthony, tomorrow could not arrive too soon. "It's a sight too bad about that smudge made by the tip of my nose, but we all have our burdens to bear," he said as lightly as the pounding of his heart would allow.

"Now, that is enough courting for one day," Grandmama insisted.

"I cannot agree, but, sadly, I haven't the time to further my cause," he said, noting out of the corner of his eye that bits and pieces of what was left of Old Q's carriage were being carried off by souvenir hunters.

"Would your need for haste have anything to do with the balloon ascension tomorrow?" Ginny asked with an arch smile.

"Ah, so you have been informed, have you?" he said, hoping he did not look as abashed as he felt.

"Indeed, rumors are flying! Do you have any other secrets you wish to share with me?" she asked, her eyes dancing.

"No!" Anthony said in all truthfulness, as least as much as he could manage at the moment. Reaching up to touch her face, he reveled in the silkiness of her skin. "However, I do have one or two surprises I warrant you will vastly enjoy," he said in a voice that sounded husky to his own ears.

"Come, now, Anthony, be off with you, or we will be eaten by flies before the hour is out!" Grandmama complained. And with that she gave the signal to her driver, and they were off.

Ginny turned to wave a time or two, but then they were gone almost as thoroughly as the carriage borrowed for the race. Making the rescue of what survived of Old Q's carriage his next task, Anthony set about mentally preparing a list of what remained. Conti was off to procure the balloon. One could only hope he knew how to operate it as well as he could tie a cravat. Better! Visions of crashing to the ground or being speared by a church spire during the journey through the sky filled him with dread. The thought of Ginny in the arms of some old goat was infinitely worse, however. There wasn't a chance Anthony would allow that to happen, powerful as his uncle was. However, Ginny might be made to believe it could happen if Anthony didn't meet his uncle's demands. One moment of believing her life would be lived as wife to a gummy old stranger was one moment too long.

Next were the carefully censored instructions for Grandmama. She must have the note for the duke, of course, but she must also be persuaded to return to Dunsmere at first light without knowing his reasons for the request. He would send a messenger ahead to Dunsmere this afternoon carrying instructions for her enlightenment upon her arrival. Meanwhile, he daren't risk news of his plans to reach the ears of Society.

Last on the list was proper wedding attire. Ginny must have her wedding gown—on that he was positively determined. He would be just as happy to marry her in the gray linsey gown with the stretched-out hem as anything else, but he suspected that Ginny had dreamed of her wedding day since she was a young girl, and gray linsey-woolsey gowns had no part in it. Once Conti had returned from his current task, he would send him off to Hertfordshire to run Madame Badeau to ground and procure the dress.

This left only his own clothing to acquire. The bespeaking of a new suit of cerulean-blue silk, very fine, a new shirt, and several neck cloths all bearing a bit more lace than Mr. Brummel would have approved, had been his first task upon arriving in London less than a week prior. It would be the work of a moment to stop at his tailor's to fetch them and purchase a new hat, as well.

There was a time when the thought of entering a haberdashery or any public place in all his dirt would have brought him to his knees. No longer. In truth, his pride in his wardrobe that once he valued above all things had fallen a notch or two in his esteem.

By the time he had returned the carriage, caught a hackney to his tailor's, headed for home, then turned around in order to procure a special license, then to finally arrive at his rooms on Jermyn Street, Conti had returned with news of the balloon.

"All ees well! I have arranged for the balloon to be brought to Regent's Park and inflated early een the morning. It shall be tethered and waiting when we arrive."

"Very good. Now, I'm afraid I have bad news for you, my man. I shall need you to rescue a princess from a tower," Anthony said wryly.

"Theese is the work of a moment!" Conti proclaimed with a snap of his fingers.

"Not when the princess is interred in Hertfordshire. I'm

afraid. In fact, I don't expect to see you again until the wee hours of the morning."

Conti pursed his lips and eyed his master narrowly. "Will you be going out again tonight?"

"Why, yes, I find that I must," Anthony replied with some surprise.

"Then I shall draw you a bath before I depart, though I am afraid I cannot linger to tie you a proper cravat," Conti said with a sigh.

"I expect that pile of neck cloths you've already ironed and I will deal famously together."

Conti merely sniffed and quit the room in search of hot water.

While waiting for his bath, Anthony scratched one word on a piece of paper and readied it for evening, when he would bring it around to Grandmama himself. He did not relish attempting to explain to her why it was so important that she arise at the crack of dawn and hasten to Dunsmere for no reason that he could explain. In the end, he found he was quite right.

"But, Anthony, we are here in London to arrange your wedding! Why would I wish to leave now?" Grandmama queried.

"I wish I could say, but I'm afraid I cannot. However, I can say that if you follow my instructions to the letter, you shall be satisfied with the outcome."

"'Instructions'? 'Outcome'?" Grandmama cried, her face turning an alarming shade of puce. "I am persuaded you have forgotten to whom you are speaking, my boy!"

"Not at all!" Anthony insisted. "You are not one who is easily forgotten. What's more, you shall be given your full due before the week is out. Now, do be a dear, and be sure to hang on to this letter until you get to Dunsmere. Do not let it out of your sight."

"But it is addressed to your uncle," she spluttered. "Why should I take it with me when you might deliver it into his hands this very night?"

"All shall be revealed in time. Once arrived, you will find a letter that will explain everything."

"So, I am not to know what any of this is about until I arrive at Dunsmere?"

"Exactly."

"Then I suppose the sooner I ready myself for departure, the better," she said, rising to her feet. "Now, off with you before I change my mind, you blackguard!"

"Good night, then. And I expect that when we meet again, it shall be in happier circumstances." He strode toward the door and paused. "I almost forgot! Have Ginny's trousseau packed up, and take it with you. And, Grandmama?"

"What is it now?" she asked with an injured air.

"You do know how very fond I am of you, do you not?"

"'Fond'? Of an old termagant such as myself?" she demanded. Before he could formulate a reply, she had thrust herself into his arms and buried her face in his chest. "I am such an old fool!"

Anthony merely held her tightly and waited.

"If I had not married your grandfather, I would have been a much happier woman. I was young and dazzled by his property and title, but it was never enough to please me. It is only now, when I see how you look at her, that I know what it is I have gone without."

"Come now, dearest," he said around the lump that had risen in his throat. "If you hadn't married my grandfather, you would not have me!"

"It's true," she said, hastily wiping away a tear. "And neither would my darling Ginerva. But she will soon be leaving me, and I do not know how I shall bear it."

"You won't have to. Once we are married, you shall come and live with us, dearest. I'm persuaded Ginny would love it above all things."

"Pshaw! To have an old lady always underfoot, telling you which way is up and which is down? I think not. Just promise me you will allow me to stay with you from time to time and that you will never, ever do anything to hurt her."

"I fear that pain is an inescapable part of love, Grandmama," he said, wishing his own heart wasn't feeling quite so bruised. "But I shall endeavor to ensure that every day of her life is a happy one."

She sighed. "With that I shall be most content."

As he had never in his life known Grandmama to be the least content, Anthony left her feeling as if he might, with a mere thought, conquer the world. His heart was lighter than it had been since that day he spied Lady Derby outside his uncle's house. Though it had seemed at the time that she was there to find a new husband in the future Duke of Marcross, it was now as clear as crystal that her target had most likely been the current duke all along. Perhaps, one day, there would be a new heir to the duchy.

It was a most welcome thought, indeed.

Chapter Seventeen

Ginny was alarmed by Grandaunt's request that she pack all they had purchased for her wedding trousseau and lay it carefully away in silver tissue for the present time.

"Has the wedding been delayed?" Ginny asked, though, truth be told, an actual date had not been discussed as of yet.

"No, I think not," Grandaunt brusquely replied. "I would simply prefer to have your new things gathered in your trunk and taken to the, er, attic, where it will be safe from housebreakers."

"Housebreakers?" Ginny asked, exchanging a puzzled look with Nan, who was to help her with the packing. "Has there been news of such here in Grosvenor Square?" Ginny asked, but Grandaunt had already bustled off to her own chamber.

With a heavy heart, Ginny proceeded to wrap up her cherished belongings, which Nan loaded into the trunk while keeping up a stream of cheerful chatter.

"Oh, how I do love these stockings! I will never forget the wool ones we endured the endless itch of in the vicarage days."

Ginny slid them from Nan's grasp and ran her fingers over the silver-shot silk. "They were for my wedding day. But here!" she insisted, thrusting them at Nan. "You have them. I fear I shall never need them now."

"Why, miss! How can you say so?" Nan asked, aghast.

"Lord Crenshaw loves you, he does, and he is going to marry you—see if he don't!"

"Yes, he does," Ginny sadly replied. "Nevertheless, it has been days, and he still has not sent notice of our engagement to the papers. His uncle hates me and will do anything to thwart us. And then there is Lady Derby. How she would relish seeing me out of the way!"

"Maybe she would! Who wouldn't, if it meant making the path clear to Lord Crenshaw? But he would never marry her, nohow, even if you had never been born!"

"He thought he loved her once," Ginny said with a sigh. "Of course, there is also the matter of his having been here in this house, this very evening. He never even asked to see me. I can't account for any reason that would be so unless he were done with me. Now this," she said, indicating the trunk that was to go with her on her wedding journey.

Nan fingered the tiny rosebuds attached to a particularly fetching muslin bonnet. Ginny was to wear it on her wedding day, as well. All it wanted was a length of veiling to be attached to the inside, a task Ginny had insisted on doing herself. Now it looked as if it might be of no consequence whatsoever.

She looked up from the bonnet to see that Nan was weeping and trying mightily to hide it. "Oh, dearest Nan," Ginny said, "what would I do without you? Here," she said, handing Nan the bonnet. "Would you be a dear and sew in the veil while I finish up here?" Perhaps the task would give Nan as much hope as it gave Ginny to think of the bonnet complete and perfect for her wedding day.

"Yes, miss! I will do a bang-up job of it, too! See if I don't!" Nan said fiercely, whereupon she retired to the sewing room to do as she was bid.

Ginny completed the packing and informed Garner that the trunk was ready to be taken to the attic as instructed. When she returned upstairs and walked past her grandaunt's bedchamber, she heard the sounds of drawers being opened and closed as her grandaunt paced back and forth. Wondering what it was she could be looking for, Ginny returned to her own room.

She was exhausted and longed for her bed, but there was still the matter of the trunk to be fetched from her room. While she waited for the boot boy to come and take it away, she picked up a book she had purchased at Hatchard's during her shopping trip the day prior. The novel was called *Pamela, or, Virtue Rewarded* by a Mr. Samuel Richardson and was set, of all places, in Bedfordshire, home to her beloved Dunsmere, where she hoped to marry Anthony in the rose garden come June.

She owned that she had much sympathy for Pamela. She was a young girl of no means and a family of no social standing who was in love with a man above her station. As Ginny read, she shuddered when it seemed as if Pamela was to be married off to an utter stranger and thought it strangely exciting when she was kidnapped and whisked away to a tower by the hero of the novel. Once Ginny's trunk had finally been removed with the newly completed bonnet safely inside, she had Nan help her out of her gown, whereupon she put on her nightgown and went to sleep with visions of rescue swimming in her head.

Ginny awoke early the next morning to the sounds of a carriage being loaded with luggage. She hopped out of bed and ran to the window that overlooked the mews at the back of the house. It was difficult to see clearly, as the sun hadn't fully risen, but Ginny was certain it was Grandaunt's traveling barouche that was being readied for departure. Wherever could she be going so early in the morning and at such short notice? And what of the wedding? Had Anthony changed his mind? Was he to marry Lady Derby instead?

Throwing on her dressing gown, she flew down the hall to her grandaunt's room and pounded on the door. "Grandaunt Regina!" she cried. "Please open the door, please! Won't somebody tell me what's happening?"

"Yes, miss, I shall be happy to be of service," Garner said, looking more cheerful than anyone had a right to be and holding out a silver salver with a note. Quickly she snatched it and tore open the seal. The Crenshaw seal. Anthony's seal.

My Beloved,
   Never fear, all shall be well. Put on your gayest gown and that fetching bonnet you sported yesterday, and be at Regent's Park by ten of the clock. Nan and Garner shall accompany you.
                                            As Ever,
                                            Your Anthony

It was as if night had broken into full day in the space of a moment. "Nan!" she cried as she ran back to her room. "Nan, fetch me my primrose-yellow sprigged muslin with the spring-green sashing! Oh, and do be sure to check that my half boots are clean and, if not, fetch me the saffron dancing slippers. On second thought, forget the boots entirely. I shall make do very well with the slippers. And *where* is that bonnet I wore yesterday?" she asked, tearing one thing after the other from the clothespress and tossing them away with abandon. "He asked for it most particularly!"

"'He' who?" Nan asked as she followed along behind her mistress, rescuing orphaned slippers, chip straw bonnets, and yards of satin sashing from the floor.

"*He* who, that's who! Oh, Nan!" Ginny cried, forcing a pile of muslin gowns into Nan's already full arms. "You don't know! You are to come along, so we must hurry if we are to get both of us turned out as fine as a new penny before it is time to leave. First we must have breakfast, though I must own, I'm not the least bit hungry. Then we must curl our hair, and it shall be left to you to iron the gowns, as I daresay Grandaunt's abigail has gone off in the barouche, but it's not of the least consequence, as she has a tendency to scorch things, a fact about which Grandaunt hasn't the least idea, as she never wears anything but that abysmal black!" she said without so much for pausing for air. "Then, as long as we can find where I tossed my bonnet yesterday, we shall be ready!"

"Yes, miss, but where is it we are going?" Nan asked, her eyes wide.

"Oh, naturally, you would have no way of knowing! It's all here in this note," Ginny said, thrusting the paper at Nan to read.

"But this doesn't say where," Nan complained.

"Do pardon me, Nan. I am all at sixes and sevens, it seems!"

Taking Ginny by the shoulders, Nan steered her toward the bed and sat her down. "Now, tell me, where are we going?"

Ginny folded her hands primly in her lap and tried to contain her excitement. "I believe we are going to a wedding."

"A weddin'?" Nan said with a frown. "Whose weddin'?"

"Mine, you silly goose," Ginny said, rising from the bed and beginning to dance about the room. "Don't you see? It all fits! My gown is gone, so he has asked me to wear my best, though truly my white satin ball gown is much finer. Still, I shan't wear it, for it is much too warm. Grandaunt is also gone. Doubtless she is in on the surprise and has headed off to where the wedding shall take place. She ordered that my trousseau be packed up—an odd request under the circumstances, wouldn't you agree?"

"Well, yes, I suppose I do."

"And he has sent me a note to ensure I will arrive in plenty of time, when he was so against me even being the least aware of the boxing match or the carriage race!"

"But, if it's to be your weddin', why *wouldn't* he want you there on time?"

"Because, silly, it's not a wedding! It's a balloon ascension!"

"I see," Nan said, looking as puzzled as ever. "I shall just go and see if I have anything suitable for a balloon ascension turned weddin' in my clothespress, then," she added and departed.

When they arrived at Regent's Park, carefully dressed, coiffed, hatted, sashed, and shod, they were taken aback by the sight of an enormous hot-air balloon made of gaily colored silks and encased in netted roping, which was in turn attached to a large basket painted blue and gold. If it were possible, the crowd gathered today was larger than for the race. Carriages of every description reached as far as the eye could see, and there were throngs of people of all walks of life sitting and standing on every available surface. Some had even made themselves comfortable in trees, including one lady of dubious reputation whose fast gown and forward ways caused Ginny to blush.

"Here we are, miss. According to my instructions, you are to alight from the carriage, and I shall assist you in making your way to the balloon," Garner said.

"I see I am to have the best of accommodations," Ginny quipped, sinking into a gilt chair on the lawn near the base of the balloon. What the rest of the day held in store, she didn't see at all, but she had to own that it was all very exciting.

She hadn't long to wait before the masses parted and the most beloved face she had ever known emerged from the crowd. He was wearing her favorite outfit, a dark blue coat over buff pantaloons and just a bit of lace at the throat and wrists. No matter how staid men's fashions became, she fervently hoped lace would not altogether fade from a gentleman's wardrobe.

He greeted Nan and Garner and, taking Ginny by the hand, raised her to a standing position. Together they walked, arm in arm, until they stood with the balloon at their backs and faced the crowd. Cheers rent the air, but the moment he placed his foot on the wooden steps that led to the balloon's interior, an impossible hush fell like a blanket over the crowd.

"One and all, I thank you for being here today! I would also thank you to hold your cheering until I have completed my speech, at which time you might shout until you are hoarse!"

As his words were met by a hearty roar, Ginny rather doubted that Anthony would have much success in keeping order. However, whistles and other injunctions to hush followed, and presently it was quiet enough for him to proceed.

"I am Lord Crenshaw, and this maiden by my side is my affianced bride!"

"So, this is to be an engagement party?" Ginny shouted to Anthony over the fresh din. "I daresay I am the only girl in England whose betrothal has been announced at a balloon ascension!"

"Shh!" he said, putting his finger to her lips. "I believe Lady Derby's engagement to her dead earl was announced at a balloon ascension, more's the pity, so *I* shall do you one better!" Climbing to the very top step, he waved his arms for silence. "In celebration of my impending marriage to Miss Delacourt, I have provided food and drink in the tents on the far side of the park."

The roar that followed that pronouncement was one unlike Ginny had ever before heard. The people turned, seemingly en masse, and headed for the proffered food.

"Why ever did you do that?" she asked. "I thought they came to see the balloon go up."

"They did," he replied as he moved back down the steps. "However, I needed a diversion so that I could do *this*," he said, and, taking her bodily into his arms, he bore her quickly up the steps, depositing her neatly into the balloon. "You don't know how I sorrow to ask this of you, my darling, but you must crouch, so none will be the wiser as to your presence."

Ginny obediently sank down on her heels and attempted not to giggle, an endeavor most difficult to accomplish, especially in light of the startling proximity of Conti's nose to hers.

"Are you to be a witness, then?" Ginny whispered.

"Eet ees not for me to say, Meess Delacourt, but I wish you every happiness."

"Do stop turning my bride up sweet, Conti, and move aside," Anthony scolded. Climbing into the balloon, he proceeded to follow Conti's instructions to the letter until, with a loud whoosh, they were aloft.

"Now, Ginny, you must stay unseen, more's the pity, until I say the word," Anthony insisted.

She was beginning to enjoy herself as she never had before. "Am I being abducted like Pamela?" she teased.

"Yes, and you shall like it better than she, I warrant!"

"What of Conti? I am persuaded I have never seen so much black folded up into such a small space."

"Thees is a tragedy of no little consequence, meess, and the master shall pay for a new suit when thees ees done!" Conti averred.

Ginny laughed. "But why?"

"It was necessary that I fly the balloon myself for reasons I shall presently explain," Anthony replied. "However, there was not time for Conti to instruct me on the niceties, and even had he done so, I fear I shall never get us to our destination without him. There, I think we are far enough above the ground to hide your presence," he said, taking her hand and helping her to rise.

Ginny's hopes to survey the surrounding countryside from the air were temporarily delayed, for the moment she was on her feet, she found herself crushed in an unyielding pair of arms and hungrily kissed. She felt scandalous all the way down to her toes, but there was nothing for it but to surrender to the sweetness of it and count her blessings that Conti had a view only of their properly clad feet.

Eventually the sound of Conti's snoring wakened them from their reverie.

"Poor Conti," Anthony drawled. "I had him out until all hours of the morning and then up before the crack of dawn. But it was for a good cause."

"Oh? What, pray tell, is a better cause then to fly through the air with my love?" Ginny said, drawing her fingers down the side of his face, an action that apparently delighted him to no end, for she was not to hear the answer to her question until after another splendidly thorough kiss.

Finally, with a sigh, Anthony took a step back and pulled a parcel from the bottom of the basket. "I could not bear the thought of wedding you without the gown you so well adore," he said, handing her the parcel. "I can only hope you will adore your groom half as well!"

Ginny felt a surge of joy. "This is my gown? The one Madame Badeau made up for me?"

"If by 'Madame Badeau' you mean one Miss James of Stevenage, Hertfordshire, yes. It seems she fancied the gown for her own nuptials slated to occur a fortnight hence and will instead wed in some hastily made-up costume of inferior quality, no doubt."

"Oh, Anthony!" Ginny cried, throwing her arms around him. "Now everything shall be absolutely perfect, since, I feel free to assume, my trunk went ahead with Grandaunt Regina this morning?"

"Where else?" he asked. "But, if I am not mistaken, there are one or two other questions you are burning to ask, just as I am burning to answer them."

Ginny tilted her head and studied his face, wondering if they could possibly be speaking of the same questions. "Very well, then. Why the boxing match, the carriage race, and now this delicious balloon?"

"You are shockingly predictable, my dear, but very well," he said with a sigh. "My uncle, the duke, was determined to make things difficult for us. At first it was because he was dying and feeling thwarted, so he found he must thwart as many others as possible. Other than his unfortunate servants, he has more power over his heir than most anyone. As you might have noticed, however, he seems to have made a full recovery. In fact, I fully expected to see him here today, but I did not. I suspect his most recent motivation for insisting on these tasks falls in line with the reason he was not in attendance."

"And what might that be, pray tell?"

"Yes, of course. But first I need to tell you why I went along with his demands. Surely you would never believe I would give you up simply because my uncle was proving difficult?"

"No," she said with a proud lift of her chin. "But I did fear that his disapproval, along with your mother's and that of Society's, might dampen your ardor. Then, when I saw Lady Derby . . . well, I found I could not feel utterly confident."

Taking both of her hands in his, he drew them to his heart. "Ah, darling Ginny, if I had thought for one moment your knowledge of her would cause you pain, I would not have breathed a word about her. Just know that I was very young, too young to know my own heart. Lady Derby, on the other hand, doesn't have one. I once believed I would never see the day when I would be grateful for her utter lack of feeling, but when I look into your eyes and try to imagine my life without you, I am forever grateful that she so cruelly turned me away."

There was little response to that which wasn't better said with a kiss, but eventually Ginny remembered there were more questions remaining.

"If it were all that simple, why, then, did you not tell me what was happening?"

"Ah! Here we come to the meat of the matter—indeed, the part about which I am not so proud. At first I went along with it because it seemed simple enough to accomplish, and I felt I required some leverage in dealing with my uncle. Yet I thought better of informing you how matters stood, as I had no wish to worry you. You spent so much time weeping as it was! Then, once my uncle sent those two snakes to spread the word about, and wagers were made, I felt that I could not back out of it without the whole world knowing. My darling, I would have taken you off and wed you a dozen times over these last few days if it weren't for the fear that, upon our return to London, your ears would be filled with talk of your husband's cowardice or, worse yet, that you were something of which to be ashamed."

Ginny pulled her hands away from his chest and nestled her head in their place. It was surprisingly cold up in the balloon, and his arms willingly came up and around to warm her, as she knew they would.

"So, we are to be married in the rose garden at Dunsmere. And to think, today is the first of June! Baldwin will be so happy!"

"Baldwin? Who is this Baldwin?" Anthony asked in feigned fury.

"He is Grandaunt's gardener. Ever since I came to live with her, he has often said how he's been growing the roses for my wedding day. Is that not the sweetest thing?" she asked, tilting her head back to look into his eyes.

"No, my love. *You* are the sweetest thing! Well, except when you are angry and there are sharp things about."

Ginny laughed and then bethought herself of a tantalizing bit of information he had mentioned earlier. "And what of your uncle? Why is it that he truly wants you to busy yourself with these unreasonable tasks, and why would he miss the balloon ascension?" Having seen him out and about with Lady Derby on several occasions, Ginny thought she knew the answer, but she wanted to hear it from her beloved's own lips.

He gave a gusty sigh so large, her head bobbed back and forth against his chest. "I believe it was all a grand diversion and that he has eloped with Lady Derby, a rather scandalous act, when one considers she has been a widow slightly longer than a year. Which brings to mind my last question, dearest, and you must answer this honestly. How fond were you of becoming a duchess one day?"

Slipping from his arms, she took his face between her hands. "Oh, my darling, let us pray that the new Duchess of Marcross will wax fruitful and multiply!"

He smiled, a wide, joyous grin. "So, you weren't any fonder of the idea of being a duchess than I was of being a duke?"

"Why, Anthony, how could you have doubted? Money, titles, and, as handsome as you look in them, clothes . . . they are all just a façade." Placing her arms around his neck, she kissed him on the cheek. "All I have ever wanted is you, the man behind the mask."

Epilogue

"Why, listen to this, my flower," Lord Avery exclaimed one morning in June. "It says here in the society page that Anthony, Lord Crenshaw, and Miss Ginerva Delacourt were married in Bedfordshire a fortnight past."

Lucinda made a little moue. "I wonder that we were not invited! How odd, for I am persuaded we are their only friends. If I were she, I would be most happy to have an earl and countess attend my wedding."

"Yes, my darling, but there is more. It says they were married by special license in a rose garden, of all places!"

"And to think we were married at that moldy hotel in Gretna Green!" Lucinda exclaimed. "How I should have liked to have married by special license, instead. I am told they cost the earth!"

"But, Lucinda, my love, there was no time to obtain one. As you may recall, we were being held captive in your house due to that pox quarantine."

"Yes, of course, but I am persuaded that some flowers would have been lovely. Ginny had a whole garden of them!"

Lord Avery sighed and carried on. "The groom wore a suit of blue silk, and the bride, a gown of the finest white muslin embroidered all over with tiny rosebuds. The skirt was done up in a triple layer of ruching and adorned with silk in palest rose. In addition, her bonnet was most becoming, with a layer of veiling to frame the bride's face."

"I want a dress of the finest white muslin," Lucinda said with a pout.

"You already possess a quantity of white muslin dresses, my love!" Lord Avery countered.

"Yes, but now that we are married, I am expected to wear colors everywhere I go!"

"But, my darling! You said you were sick unto death of white and could hardly wait to be a married woman so that you might wear any color you chose!"

"I find that I was wrong, Eustace. If you loved me, you would annul our marriage on the spot!"

"Lucinda, you know I cannot do that! However, I will own that it pinches a bit to read of other weddings when our own was so paltry. I know! We shall have a ball, and you will have a dress made up as fine as you wish. I shall bespeak every blossom in town, and there will be candles, the glow of which will rival Carlton House!"

"Oh, yes!" Lucinda cried. "I should like to invite the Prince Regent and show him how much brighter and better and thinner we are than he!"

"Then it is settled," Lord Avery said, returning to his newspaper.

"Eustace?"

"Yes, my love?"

"Do you suppose they are thinking of us at all?"

"Who? Do you mean to say Crenshaw and Ginny?"

"Yes, them."

"No, my love," he said, patting her hand. "Doubtless they are not giving us a passing thought."

At that very moment, Ginny, in a smart new gown of pomona-green silk, and her adored husband, head bare and coat abandoned, were floating in a gondola in Venice. This was her favorite time of day, made wholly better by the sight of her Anthony poling them along the river with his sleeves rolled up past his elbows, browned arms glistening in the sun.

From time to time they were content to float free, and Anthony would take his place by the side of his beloved wife and quote poetry.

"Do please recite that one, Anthony!"

"Which one is that?" he asked with an idle air, engrossed in curling one of her silky locks around his fingers.

"I'm persuaded you know just the one I mean! It is my favorite above all of Shakespeare's sonnets, the one that claims "rough winds do shake the darling buds of May."

"Ah, yes, *that* one." Leaning close to gaze into her shining eyes, he began.